WHAT HAPPE

Jay Northcote

Copyright

Cover artist: Garrett Leigh.
Editor: Sue Adams.
What Happens at Christmas © 2015 Jay Northcote.

ALL RIGHTS RESERVED

This literary work may not be reproduced or transmitted in any form or by any means, including electronic or photographic reproduction, in whole or in part, without express written permission.
This is a work of fiction and any resemblance to persons, living or dead, or business establishments, events or locales is coincidental.
The Licensed Art Material is being used for illustrative purposes only.
All Rights Are Reserved. No part of this may be used or reproduced in any manner whatsoever without written permission, except in the case of brief quotations embodied in critical articles and reviews.

Warning
This book contains material that is intended for a mature, adult audience. It contains graphic language, explicit sexual content, and adult situations.

CHAPTER ONE

Justin groaned inwardly as he skimmed the email reminding him and his colleagues of the details for the office Christmas party the following weekend. This was exactly why getting involved with a co-worker had been a terrible plan. Partners were invited, and he knew that Andy wouldn't pass up the opportunity to show off his new boyfriend.

"Oh, it sounds like it's going to be a good one this year," Jess said from her desk, where she was obviously reading the same message that had just pinged into more than one hundred inboxes at the finance company they worked for. "One of my mates works at the hotel they've hired for it, and it's really fancy. The food should be great."

"Yeah." Justin tried to inject some enthusiasm into his tone.

From the way Jess looked up sharply, he obviously failed.

"Justin, you are going to come, aren't you?"

He shrugged. "I'm not sure I can face it."

He'd been trying his best to avoid Andy since the split. Luckily they worked in different departments, so their paths didn't cross too often.

Jess's expression softened, but there was a thread of steel in her voice. "You've already paid for your ticket, though. Don't let him do this. Please come, Justin. Show him you're having a good time without him in your life. It will be fun. Plus, Kieran is coming, and I'm sure he has a crush on you."

Justin managed a smile at that. Kieran was a new guy, who had started in their department a few weeks ago. "Really? He's sweet, but he's not my type."

"Yeah." Jess sighed. "I had a feeling he wouldn't be. You like them tall, dark, and handsome." Kieran was cute and blond—much like Justin himself.

It was true. Justin had always been drawn to tall guys with dark hair, and if they had brown eyes like melted chocolate, then so much the better. Justin preferred not to think about why he had such an instaboner for guys who looked like that. Andy had ticked all Justin's boxes physically. Shame he'd turned out to be an arsehole who couldn't keep it in his pants.

"So, will you come? It won't be the same without you," Jess said hopefully.

"I'll think about it."

"*Please.*"

"I said I'll think about it. Okay?" He felt like a heel for snapping at Jess, but she was poking at a splinter, and it hurt.

"Fine, fine." She held up her hands and went back to her spreadsheets.

By the time Justin was on his way home that evening, his spirits had lifted a little despite the fight through the Friday rush-hour crowds on the London Underground. For the first time since he'd split up with Andy, he wasn't going to be spending the weekend under his duvet with Netflix for company, because Sean was coming to stay.

Tall-dark-and-handsome Sean with the melted-chocolate eyes—Justin's oldest friend and his unrequited crush.

Justin couldn't wait to see him. They'd known each other since they were seven, and Sean was the only person Justin was still mates with from primary school. They'd gone off to uni in separate cities, but their friendship had weathered the separation. Both of them ended up living and working in London after graduation: Justin at his current job and Sean temping. They'd shared a flat for a while, but when Sean left to go travelling for nine months, Justin had managed to get a mortgage on the place he had now—with a lot of help from his parents.

On the way home, Justin stopped at the supermarket at the end of his road and stocked up with as much food as he could carry. His fridge had been pathetically bare for the last two weeks, as he'd had no appetite. He'd survived on a diet of breakfast cereal with the occasional slice of toast for variety. But unless Sean had changed while he'd been away, he loved his food, and the contents of Justin's cupboards just wouldn't cut it.

Laden down with bags of groceries, Justin was struggling to get his key in the front door of his building when a voice from behind him said, "Justin? Is that you?"

It was a voice Justin would know anywhere. He turned, letting the bags slip from his hands to the floor, barely noticing when one of them fell over and a couple of tins of beans made a bid for freedom.

"Sean?" Justin could just make out the shape of his friend in the orange glow of the street lamps, a bulging rucksack on his back.

"God, it's good to see you."

Sean moved forward and Justin went to meet him. They wrapped their arms around each other for a hug that went on for ages.

Sean was big and solid, and warm compared to the early December chill. He smelled as though he hadn't had a shower in a couple of days, but Justin didn't care. He squeezed back until Sean finally let him go.

"I thought you weren't coming till tomorrow," Justin said.

"Yeah, sorry. Is it a bad time? I managed to switch to an earlier flight."

"It's fine." Justin shivered, chilly now he was out of Sean's warm arms. "Let me get the door."

He fumbled with his keys again, and once he got the front door open, the automatic light in the hall came on so he could see to pick up the shopping.

"Here." Sean handed him the tins that had rolled away. "God. I haven't seen real baked beans for months. It's good to be home."

Justin chuckled. "Seriously?"

"Seriously. It's funny the things you miss when you're abroad."

Justin led Sean inside. "Make sure the door's shut behind you, it sometimes sticks. My flat's on the first floor."

They made their way up the stairs, where the carpet was worn and grimy from use.

"This is me." Justin unlocked the first of two doors on the landing and went in, with Sean following.

Justin flipped on the light. He studied Sean now he could see him clearly. His tall frame looked a lot thinner than before he went away and his cheekbones were more defined, emphasising his strong features. His face was tanned, jaw dark with stubble, and his hair a little longer than he usually wore it. It suited him. Justin's breath caught as a wave of affection and longing swept through him. All these years, and the feelings he guarded so closely still persisted.

Sean smiled, and Justin realised he was staring.

"The beach-bum look suits you," he said casually, ignoring the flush heating his cheeks.

"Thanks. Where shall I put this?" Sean asked, easing his giant rucksack off his shoulders.

"Oh, just dump it anywhere for now. Let me get this shopping into the kitchen, and I'll give you a tour—not that it will take long."

Justin's one-bedroom flat was tiny, but it was home and he loved it.

"So this is the living room, obviously," Justin said as they walked through it. "And the kitchen's in here." The kitchen was small but functional. It led directly off the living room, separated by a door. Justin put the shopping bags on the counter and started unpacking the fridge stuff.

"This is great, Justin," Sean said. He was still standing in the kitchen doorway, looking around admiringly. "And it's all yours?"

"Well, I've got a mortgage, of course, but it's not astronomical. My parents were able to give me a good-size deposit when they sold their place to move to Scotland."

"That's very cool. I'm already stressing about finding somewhere to live if I want to stay in London. Rent is crazy, and I need a job first."

"You're welcome to stay as long as you need," Justin said. "You know that."

"You say that now... but I'm pretty sure you'll get tired of me. I'm really messy, and I fart a lot."

Justin laughed. "You don't need to tell me that. I remember. And when we were at school, you always tried to blame your farts on me."

"The one who smelt it dealt it."

Justin threw a bag of Doritos at Sean's head, but Sean caught them — and then opened them and started eating. Sean grinned obnoxiously, mouth full of orange cheesiness, and Justin tried to glare but couldn't pull it off. His heart swelled, and he felt happy for the first time since Andy had dumped him. It was so good to have Sean back.

Once Justin had put the shopping away, he showed Sean the rest of the flat. "This is the bathroom. The shower's over the bath, but it's pretty good. And my bedroom's this one." He went through the final door that led off the hallway. "It's a mess. I was going to tidy up, but you turned up early."

"I'm shocked and appalled." Sean shook his head in mock disapproval as he looked around the bedroom. A pile of clothes spilled off an armchair in the corner, and the bed was crumpled and unmade. "Seriously, man. You should see some of the places I crashed in over the last few months. This is nothing."

"You can tell me your horror stories later. You've hardly updated your blog since the summer. I can't wait to hear all about it. Rather you than me, by the sound of it. I like my home comforts or nice hotel beds."

Justin picked up Sean's rucksack on their way back through the hall.

"Holy crap, Sean. This weighs a ton. What have you got in here, rocks?" Justin could barely lift it one-handed. He let it drop in the living room next to the sofa. "Here's your bed. It pulls out into a double. It's quite comfortable, apparently. Not that I've slept on it myself."

"Brilliant." Sean yawned, stretching and rubbing his eyes. "I'm knackered. I hardly slept on the plane. Add that to the eight-hour time difference, and I'm going to pass out pretty soon. Sorry, I'm going to be crap company tonight."

"Want some food before you crash?"

Sean rubbed his stomach thoughtfully. "Yeah. I probably should, but something light. I'm not hungry because my body thinks it's 3:00 a.m., but you're supposed to try and get back in sync as soon as you land."

"Beans on toast?" Justin offered, remembering Sean's excitement at seeing good old British baked beans earlier.

"Hell yes. I've had nothing but noodles and rice for the last week in Singapore. I'm ready for something that tastes like home. Have you got any brown sauce?"

"Of course."

"This is why you're my best friend ever." Sean grinned.

"Yeah, yeah. Cupboard love." Justin couldn't help smiling back. "It's good to have you back. Welcome home."

They ate their dinner sitting on the sofa, while Sean regaled Justin with stories of his travels. He'd worked his way around Australia and New Zealand for most of it, staying on farms for bed and board and spending his savings on the travel. But he'd kept aside enough to visit Hong Kong, Thailand, and Singapore on his way home.

"Hong Kong is crazy. So many people crammed into a tiny space, buildings reaching up to the sky. But it's awesome. So much life, so vibrant. I loved it there."

"It sounds amazing," Justin said wistfully. He'd never travelled outside Europe—if you could even call the Eurocamp holidays he'd had with his parents travelling. "I want to go to places like that one day."

"You should." Sean yawned hugely. "Save up your holiday and take three weeks sometime. You won't regret—" Another yawn cut off his words.

"Bedtime?" Justin suggested. It wasn't even eight o'clock yet, but Sean was slurring as though he was drunk, and he was only drinking water.

"I reckon." Sean looked rueful. "Sorry. I haven't even had a chance to ask what's going on with you. But honestly, I think if you tell me now, I won't remember it tomorrow anyway. I've reached that point where my brain is too tired to work anymore."

"You go and get ready. I'll make the bed up for you."

"You're an angel." Sean stood, picking up his plate and Justin's and taking them into the kitchen before coming back to rummage around in his rucksack. Wash kit in hand, he asked, "Can I borrow a towel? I have one of those travel ones, but it's a bit manky."

"In the cupboard in the bathroom," Justin said.

"Thanks. If I'm not out in ten minutes, I've probably fallen asleep in your shower, so come and rescue me before I drown."

Justin laughed. "Will do."

Sean was back in less than five. He arrived on a waft of toothpaste and shampoo, hair still damp from the shower and a towel wrapped around his hips. "That's better," he said. "But I'm so knackered I forgot to take any clean clothes in with me." He stooped to dig around in his rucksack again. Then, completely unselfconsciously, he dropped his towel and stepped into his boxers.

His back was towards Justin, so Justin allowed himself the luxury of looking. The bumps on Sean's spine were clearly visible; he'd definitely lost weight while he was travelling. But God, Sean still had a gorgeous arse. It had been a few years since Justin had seen it in all its bare-skinned glory. Now it was a little furrier than Justin remembered, soft-looking dark hairs sprinkled the globes of his buttocks, thickening on his thighs and down his legs.

Justin tore his gaze away quickly, ashamed of himself for ogling his friend. Not that Sean would care, probably. But although they were both gay, they'd never been anything other than friends, and after so many years of trying to fight his attraction to Sean, it still felt wrong to think of him that way.

When Justin turned back, Sean was dressed in a long-sleeved T-shirt and threadbare sweatpants. Justin watched as he sat on the edge of the now made-up bed and pulled on thick socks.

"I do have central heating, you know." Justin raised an eyebrow, teasing, as Sean looked up.

Exhaustion was written in every line and shadow of his face. Purple marks as dark as bruises smudged under dark eyes glazed with tiredness.

"Yeah. But I've come from the tropics. Believe me. I'll need the layers for a couple of days at least."

He got into the bed and snuggled down under the duvet.

"Goodnight, then."

"Night," Sean replied.

Justin left, turning the light out on his way. In his room, he took the extra blanket off his own bed and padded back quietly to where Sean was sleeping. He spread the blanket over Sean, making sure it was pulled up to cover him.

Sean's breathing was slow and steady, and he didn't stir.

"In case you get cold," Justin whispered. "Sleep well."

CHAPTER TWO

Sean woke and opened his eyes to almost total darkness. Disorientated, he lay still for a moment, trying to remember where he was. He'd slept in so many different places in the past few months, the mental stocktake of *Where the fuck am I?* was familiar.

He was warm, snug under layers of bedding. That was new. The air that touched his face was cool, nothing like the humid tropical heat he was used to. The last twenty-four hours replayed in his mind: airports and queues, a godawful thirteen-hour flight, more airports, more queues, followed by the special hell of navigating the London Underground during the rush hour with a massive rucksack. Then arriving at Justin's flat, an oasis of calm after the insanity of travelling.

It was so good to see him. Sean smiled into the dark as he remembered Justin greeting him last night and the easy way they'd slipped back into their friendship, like putting on a comfortable old pair of shoes. He didn't realise how much he'd missed Justin till he had him back.

Wide awake now, Sean sat up. He had no idea what time it was. Where the fuck had he put his phone last night? The battery was probably flat, anyway. He squinted at the clock on the TV box across the room. 2:07 a.m.

Hello, jet lag, my old friend.

He sighed. Even though his brain was dull with sleep deprivation, he knew there was no way he was going to be able to go back to sleep for a while. He got out of bed and carefully felt his way across the room to the door to find the light switch.

"Shit," he cursed as glaringly bright light flooded the room. He squinted, looking around till he saw a smaller lamp in the corner and turned that on instead, then stumbled back to turn the overhead light off.

He dug his phone out of his jeans pocket and put it on to charge, then found the TV remote and spent a few minutes trying to work out how Justin's TV system worked. He managed to open Netflix and settled back into the bed, propped up on pillows. It was time to find out how many episodes of *Arrested Development* he could watch before he was ready to sleep again.

Sean never found out because he lost count after the first four. But at some point he must have fallen asleep again because the next thing he knew was the *click* of the door and the creak of footsteps.

"Ugh," Sean groaned, cranking his eyes open to see daylight filtering through too-thin curtains. Justin stood by the side of the sofa bed, his bleached blond hair mussed from sleep and sticking up oddly at the back. "Whassa time?"

The TV was still playing, chattering away to itself.

"Half nine," Justin replied. "Sorry. I didn't want to wake you, but I'm hungry and getting kind of desperate for some coffee." He smiled, dimples denting his cheeks.

"'S okay." Sean rubbed his eyes, then blinked a few times, trying to will away the cotton wool that appeared to have taken residence in his brain. "I should probably try and get up now anyway, given that it's daytime. Fuck, I feel rough."

"You look it." Justin sounded sympathetic. "Coffee?"

"God, yes please. A bucket of it."

"Coming right up."

Sean didn't have the energy to move far, but he hauled himself up into a position that was more sitting than lying, turned the TV off, and listened to Justin pottering around in the kitchen.

When Justin returned, Sean laughed when he saw the size of the mug he held out. It must have easily held a pint, if not more.

"I wasn't expecting you to take me so literally."

"I've never used it before. It was a stupid free promo mug that came with a delivery from Sports Direct and I never got around to chucking it. I'm glad it's finally come in handy."

Sean lifted it and took a sip. "Awesome." It was perfect. Exactly the right amount of milk and sugar. "If this doesn't wake me up, nothing will."

They had a lazy morning, chilling, eating breakfast, and playing *Call of Duty*. It was like old times, when they used to hang around at each other's houses as teenagers. But by mid-afternoon, Sean was getting sleepy again.

"I could have a power nap," he suggested. "For an hour, maybe?"

"Nope." Justin shook his head adamantly. "You said earlier that I wasn't allowed to let you sleep until at least ten o'clock tonight."

"I knew that would come back to bite me on the arse. Seriously, just half an hour, then, to take the edge off?" He put his controller aside and leaned back, closing his eyes. He could fall asleep in a matter of minutes; the pull of lethargy was like quicksand, trying to drag him under.

"No." Justin stood and grabbed Sean's hand, tugging till he opened his eyes and allowed Justin to pull him up. "Come on, we're going out. That's the only way I'll keep you awake for a few more hours."

"I hate you," Sean groaned.

"No, you don't. You love me."

Sean's heart thumped in agreement. *But just as a friend*, he reminded himself.

For years he'd tried to convince himself that his crush on his childhood friend was just that—a crush, nothing important, something he'd grow out of—but now they were together again, those feelings had come rushing back as strong as ever.

"Please tell me there'll be caffeine?" Sean said.

"For you, baby. Anything."

"Where are you taking me?" Sean asked, as they walked along Justin's street.

Sean shivered, hunching down into his coat. His beanie was pulled low over his ears, and he'd borrowed a scarf from Justin. He was still cold. The wind was bitter, carrying a hint of sleet with it.

"A café. It's not far, about twenty minutes' walk."

"Can't we get the Tube?"

"No way am I letting you get on the Tube. You'll fall asleep."

Sean had to admit Justin was probably right. He could almost fall asleep on his feet at the moment.

Maybe he could sleepwalk to wherever Justin was taking him....

"So, I haven't had a chance to catch up on what's going on with you," Sean said. "How's the job going? Are you still happy with it?"

"Yeah. I like the work. It's interesting most of the time. I'm still a total dogsbody who has to pick up all the jobs nobody else wants to do, but at least I'm getting some experience."

"And how are things with Andy?" Sean deliberately kept his voice super casual. It wasn't an unreasonable question, surely? Mates talked about stuff like that.

He'd always known about Justin's boyfriends before — and had envied every single one of them — but he'd never liked Andy right from when Justin started seeing him this time last year. Sean had been gutted when Justin introduced him to Andy, because by then he was out of the closet, and he'd been thinking about finally admitting his own feelings for Justin. But with Sean saving to leave the country for nine months, the timing for a big declaration seemed all wrong, so he'd hesitated, and then Andy had swooped in and stolen Justin out from under his nose.

Once Justin and Andy were together, Andy had been hanging around their flat like a bad smell, and yes, Sean was jealous, but it was more than that. Something about Andy set Sean's teeth on edge. He'd never trusted him.

Justin's long silence clued Sean in to the fact that all wasn't well.

"Justin?" He grabbed his friend's coat sleeve and made him stop. "What happened?"

"It's over, okay? I know you never liked him, but please don't gloat about it, because it's still pretty raw."

A tiny, guilty little part of Sean couldn't help feeling pleased. He didn't think he could handle staying with Justin for long if he had to watch Justin playing happy families with Andy again. His hopes rose at the thought that finally, for the first time since they'd known each other — well, for the first time since Sean had come out, at least — the timing might be right for something to happen between them. Maybe Justin would want to rebound onto him? Sean would be okay with that.

The expression on Justin's face made Sean feel like a complete arsehole for thinking those things. Their friendship was more important.

"Well, come on, then. Tell me what happened," Sean said.

Justin pulled his arm away from Sean and started walking again, so Sean fell into step beside him.

"He'd been cheating on me for months, with various guys through a hook-up app. It wasn't till he got serious with one in particular that I finally got suspicious. I checked his phone and found out what he'd been doing."

The hurt in Justin's voice made all Sean's protective instincts stand up and roar. He'd been Justin's personal bodyguard at school for years, and any hint of someone causing Justin physical or emotional pain made Sean want to rearrange their face for them. "Fucker," he growled. "Seriously, what a total bastard. But if that's what he did to you, then you're better off without him."

"Yeah. I suppose. Doesn't make me feel any happier about it at the moment, though. He could be a lot of fun. We had a good time together while it lasted."

"It's his loss," Sean said gruffly.

"Yeah, well. You have to say that." Justin nudged him gently.

It was true though. Andy must be an idiot. "You're still pretty hung up on him then?" Sean asked.

There was a long pause. "I suppose. I mean... I know it's stupid to want him back. But I miss what we had, you know? I like being in a relationship."

Justin was a serial monogamist. He'd come out young... well, he'd never really been in the closet. With Justin, people tended to assume his sexuality, and he had eventually given up correcting people. With Sean by his side, he hadn't had too much shit for it at school. He'd managed to surround himself with friends who were supportive and ignore the haters. Justin had had his first proper boyfriend in their final year at school, which had driven Sean crazy with jealousy. Sean had still been fighting his own internal battles at the time, knowing deep down that he was gay too, but he wasn't even ready to admit it to himself, let alone anyone else. So he'd been stuck playing the part of the ladies' man, leaving a trail of broken teenage hearts behind him when he never wanted to get serious with anyone.

"Okay, here we are." Justin stopped outside a café.

"Wow."

Sean stood and stared at the exterior. It was a narrow building squeezed in between a homeware shop on one side and a vintage clothes shop on the other. Even on this colourful street of kitsch London shops, the café was the jewel in the crown, almost literally. The window frames and front door were painted shocking pink, and the windows were draped with sparkly, gauzy fabric and intertwined strings of multicoloured fairy lights and tinsel. Sean wondered whether the tinsel was a nod to the season or whether they kept it up all year round. The sign outside read "Unicorn Café," painted in black curly lettering on a rainbow background.

"I think this is the gayest place I've ever seen," Sean said in wonder.

"I know, right?" Justin grinned. "It looks like a unicorn threw up on it. But it's awesome. The atmosphere is great, and they make the best cupcakes in London, as long as you're okay with epic amounts of food colouring and edible glitter."

"Bring it on."

Inside, the decorations were just as bright and sparkly. The tables and chairs were painted all the colours of the rainbow, and completely over-the-top Christmas decorations festooned every available nook and cranny. It was busy, but luck was on their side, and they managed to grab a small table in the corner as a couple of girls were leaving. "I already know what I want," Justin said. "I'll have the deluxe hot chocolate and a piece of their rainbow cake."

"Okay. I'll go and see what I fancy, and then I can order for both of us."

Sean went up to the counter. There was a bewildering array of cakes, cupcakes, and cookies in various shapes and sizes. Sean grinned when he saw they had choc-chip cookies shaped like penises. Next to those was a plate of iced cupcakes that at first glance he mistook for roses with petals in varying shades of pink. But when he looked more closely, he realised they were vaginas with a little silver ball for the clit. He let out a snort of laughter.

An older guy behind the counter, with greying hair and a neatly trimmed beard, caught his eye and winked. "See something you like?"

"Well, normally vagina isn't my thing, but the icing version looks pretty tasty."

The guy laughed. "Same. But yeah, those are good. I can recommend them."

"I'm tempted, but I think I'll stick with the dick."

"Motto for life." The man grinned. He slid his gaze over Sean's torso, obvious appreciation on his face. Then he glanced over Sean's shoulder, and his smile turned a little rueful. "Your boyfriend doesn't like us flirting. You can tell him he's safe. I'm married, and while I might look, I won't try and touch." He showed Sean his left hand. There was a thick silver ring on his third finger.

"Oh, but—" Sean looked over his shoulder to where Justin was watching them. He raised his eyebrows and Justin ducked his head, looking at the drinks menu again. "—we're not…. It's not like that. He's just a friend."

"Yeah? My mistake. I thought he looked a little jealous." Sean filed that bit of information away, but the guy was probably mistaken. "Are you ready to order?"

"Yes, thanks." Sean gave their order and paid, putting his change in the tip jar.

"Thank you. One of our servers will bring it over soon." His eyes twinkled as he added, "Enjoy your dick."

"I always do."

Sean went back to the table, grinning. "This place is awesome."

"Glad you approve. The guys who run it are great. I want to be like them when I grow up. I think they're a couple, although Frank—the one who served you—looked like he was chatting you up, so maybe not." Justin's smile was a little tense.

"It was only a bit of harmless flirting. He told me he's married."

"Oh, right. Good for them." Justin glanced over at Frank, looking relieved.

Could Justin really have been jealous just now? Sean wondered. Surely not, if he was still pining over his ex. Sean had occasionally wondered whether Justin had a crush on him at school. That was one of the reasons Sean hadn't told Justin about his own sexuality. He was afraid that if he'd admitted it, it would have been impossible to hide his attraction to Justin. Then if Justin had been up for some experimentation.... Well, that was a whole can of worms Sean hadn't been ready to open at the time. But surely Justin would have moved on from any adolescent crush he'd been harbouring.

Justin's phone chimed with a text, interrupting Sean's train of thought.

Justin picked up his phone to read the message. "Ugh." He put the phone back down without typing a reply and ran his hands through his hair.

"What's up?"

Justin sighed. "It's our work Christmas party next weekend. I've already got a ticket, and nearly everyone in the office goes, but it's for partners as well. One of my co-workers, Jess, is bugging me to come, but I can't face it. I bet Andy's going to bring his new boyfriend. I know he's a shit and I shouldn't let him get to me, but the thought of him parading around with my replacement, and me being there on my own, isn't very appealing."

"Is it too late to find someone to take?"

"No, they don't need final numbers till Monday."

"Well, then. Take someone else and flirt like crazy in front of him. Show him you can do better and that you've already moved on."

"But I'm not ready to date. It's only been two weeks, and I'm still at the feeling-sorry-for-myself stage."

"I'll go with you," Sean offered. "I could be your date. We could pretend we've got together and are a couple now."

"Yeah?" Justin looked thoughtful. "Are you sure?"

Duh. It would hardly be much of a sacrifice to flirt with Justin all night. It would actually be a relief not to have to hide the way he felt for a change.

"Sure," Sean replied. "I think I can manage to fake that I'm arse-over-tit infatuated with you. As long as it's only for a few hours."

"Gee, thanks." Justin rolled his eyes. "You really know how to make an already-wounded ego feel better. But if you're up for it, we should totally do it. Andy was always jealous of you before you went away. He saw you as competition because we lived together and were so close. I'd love to see his face when I walk in with you on my arm. I think he'll hate it even if he's moved on."

"Okay." Sean rubbed his hands together, excited at the prospect of getting to piss off Andy. "Let's do it! Text your friend Jess back and tell her you're in—with a hot date."

CHAPTER THREE

Jess was thrilled on Monday morning when Justin told her he'd decided to come to the party after all.

"That's great!" She clapped her hands, blonde bob swinging as she bounced with excitement. "I'm so glad. Show Andy that you don't need a boyfriend to have a good time. You're a strong, confident man who doesn't need a partner to define him. I'm not bringing anyone either, so you can hang out with me and we'll have a great night."

"Yeah... um, about that." Justin cleared his throat. "I'm actually going to bring someone."

"Oh my God. You sly dog." She slapped his arm. "Who? Do I know him?"

"No, you've never met him. He's been away travelling since March. He's an old friend from way back. We've been best mates since we were kids."

"Oh, so he's not a *date* date, then." Jess's mouth drooped in disappointment at the lack of juicy gossip.

Justin looked around the cafeteria to make sure nobody else was listening to their conversation and lowered his voice. "Well... technically no. But he's going to pretend he is."

Jess huddled closer, her face animated again. "So he's going to pose as your boyfriend? To make Andy jealous?" Her eyes widened comically. "Oh! Are you trying to win him back?"

"God, no. Jess, this isn't a Hollywood romcom. That ship has sailed. Even if Andy wanted me back, I wouldn't go running just because he crooked a finger." *Would I?* he briefly wondered. "No way." He said it emphatically to convince himself as much as Jess. "But it might put his nose out of joint to see that I've got over him so quickly, especially with someone as good-looking as Sean—because Sean's really hot. Did I mention that part?"

"No! What does he look like?"

"Tall, dark, and handsome. Think Poldark crossed with Mr Darcy."

"Ooh, nice. And I presume he's gay?"

"Yes."

"Damn it. So... this superhot, gay best friend Sean. Have you and him ever...?" She raised her eyebrows as she lifted her coffee cup to her lips.

Justin felt his cheeks flush. "God, no. Never," he said. "We're friends, but that's all."

Jess studied him, and Justin's blush intensified, heating his ears. He looked down, fiddling with a napkin to give his hands something to do.

"But you fancy him." She made it a statement rather than a question, so Justin decided he could get away with not answering. Apparently he was wrong. "Don't you?"

"I did, when we were at school. But I thought he was straight then, so it was just a stupid crush. Your typical gay boy pining over his straight best friend. It's a rite of passage. But that was years ago."

"Hmm." Jess didn't sound convinced. "Why wasn't he out at school? You must have been gutted when you found out he really was gay. All that opportunity for teenage experimentation wasted."

Justin sighed. He hated remembering Sean's coming out.

It had been the one time their friendship was truly tested, during the summer after their first year at university. They'd both come back to their home town, and Sean had told Justin one night when they were walking home from the pub. Justin's initial reaction had been one of hurt betrayal. He didn't understand how Sean could have kept the secret to himself.

"How long have you known?" was his first question.

When Sean admitted he'd known for years, maybe almost as long as Justin had known he was gay. Justin felt as though he'd been punched in the stomach. He would have trusted Sean with his life, and all that time Sean had hidden something so fundamental. Something that Justin would have understood completely.

"I can't believe you didn't tell me" was all he could manage to say. "I feel as though I don't know you at all." Hot tears threatened as anger and disbelief warred with the hurt he felt.

"I'm sorry. But I wasn't ready to talk about it to anyone," Sean said. "Please, Justin. You know what my dad's like. I was so scared he'd find out if I started telling people. He still doesn't know, and I have no plans to tell him yet."

"But you could have told *me*. You know I'd never have said anything."

Sean shook his head. "It wasn't as simple as that."

"What's that supposed to mean?" Justin demanded, his voice rising. "Seriously, Sean. I get it. I understand being scared of coming out—not that I ever had much choice because people always assumed—but you could have talked to me. Even if you hadn't told anyone else. We were best friends. I can't believe you didn't trust me with this." His voice wobbled with the effort of holding back his emotions.

"I'm sorry," Sean said again. "Maybe I should have told you. But I can't change that now."

Justin didn't answer, and they walked in silence the rest of the way home.

When they got to Sean's front door, which was just around the corner from where Justin's parents lived, they stopped.

"You said we *were* best friends," Sean said, his eyes dark and hard to read in the dimly lit street. "You're still my best friend. Just so you know."

Justin stared at him, taking in the strong features that he knew almost better than his own. The face of the person he'd been half in love with ever since he hit his teens. "You're mine too," he finally said. "Even if you're a fucking idiot for keeping that from me."

"I wish I could explain it better."

"You don't need to. I get it, even if I think you're daft. Now come here, you twat." He managed a small smile as he stepped closer and pulled Sean into a hug. Sean's arms closed around him, and the hug went on for a long time. Justin breathed in the scent of Sean's hair and skin, and his heart clenched. "Welcome to the club, you giant poofter."

Sean pulled away, laughing. "Thanks... I think."

Justin punched him lightly on the shoulder. "Night, mate."

"Night."

After that, things had been okay between them on the surface, but the hurt Justin felt had taken a long time to dissipate completely. He couldn't help torturing himself with what-ifs. How might things have been different if Sean had felt able to tell him? Had Sean ever had feelings for Justin too — might he still? Justin was too scared to ask for fear of what the answer might be. If it was a no, that would sting. But if it was a yes.... Justin wasn't sure what it would mean for his relationship with his current boyfriend. On balance, he decided it was better not to know.

"Justin?"

Jess's voice dragged him back to the present. He blinked at the bright lights in the canteen and breathed in the smell of coffee, the memories fading.

"Um, yeah. It was mainly to do with his dad, I think. It was a bit of a surprise when he finally told me."

She raised her eyebrows. "I bet."

"Anyway. Like I said, we're just friends. I don't think he's ever thought about me that way."

"Well, let's hope he can do a good job of pretending he fancies the pants off you at the party, then. I can't wait to see Andy's reaction."

Justin grinned. "Yeah. I'm hoping it will annoy him a bit. At the very least, it will show him that I'm not moping around at home, crying into a tub of Ben & Jerry's every night."

"Definitely. I think it's an excellent plan."

During the week, Justin and Sean settled into a comfortable routine of cohabitation. Justin worked standard nine-to-five hours, and Sean spent his days applying for jobs online. He had told Justin his first choice would be a job in computing, but he'd take anything he could get at the moment, so he was applying for a range of graduate jobs all over the south of England. It was a quiet time of year for recruitment with Christmas approaching, but Sean had a few telephone interviews and was hoping something would come up soon. He was willing to find temp work through an agency in the New Year if he didn't get an offer before then, and in the meantime he was living off the last of his savings. He still insisted on contributing a little towards food and bills, but Justin wouldn't let him pay any rent.

"You're sleeping on the sofa. I'm not making you pay for that!" he insisted.

"If you're sure…?"

"I'm sure."

"I need to go shopping," Sean said on Thursday evening. "If you want me to impress Andy, I'm going to need something to wear that hasn't spent the last nine months rolled up in a rucksack. All my old stuff's still packed up in my dad's loft."

Justin nodded. "Good point. I hadn't thought of that. Shame you can't borrow anything of mine."

They were very different sizes. Sean was a good four inches taller, and he was broader in the shoulder than Justin, who was a slim — if you were being polite, or skinny if you weren't — five foot nine.

"Yeah, well. If you weren't such a midget…. Ouch!" A sharp dig in the ribs shut Sean up. He retaliated by wrestling Justin to the living room floor and tickling him until he was squirming and weak with laughter.

"Gibbon. *Gibbon!*" Justin yelled, sagging with relief when Sean stopped immediately and pushed up on his arms, freeing Justin from the weight of his body.

"I can't believe you remembered that." Sean chuckled, breathless from exertion.

"You never forget your safeword." Justin rolled out from under Sean, straightening his clothes.

As kids they'd spent a lot of time play-fighting, but back then Sean hadn't known his own strength and didn't always realise when Justin had had enough. One day, when they were about nine or ten years old, Justin's mum had suggested they pick a word to use when the other person—usually Justin— really did want the game to stop. For some reason neither of them could remember, they'd settled on "gibbon." They'd used it into their early teens, but it had gradually fallen into disuse when wrestling was replaced by video games or footy in the park.

Justin was standing now, and he offered a hand to Sean, who was still on the floor.

"Cheers," Sean said as Justin hauled him up. "So, about this shopping trip…."

"You can go tomorrow while I'm at work."

"I could…"

Justin raised his eyebrows waiting for the "but" he knew was coming.

"…but you know how shit I am with fashion. I'm still not allowed to dress myself."

Justin laughed. "Oh, yeah. I'd almost forgotten."

"I need to get some more clothes for everything, not just the party. I only have one pair of jeans without holes in, and most of my clothes are more suited to the tropics than London in the middle of winter. Plus I need something to wear for interviews, assuming I get some soon."

"And you want me to help you?"

"Please?" Sean gave him a hopeful grin. "You've always been great at picking stuff out for me."

As teenagers, whenever they'd had spare cash to spend on clothes, they'd always gone shopping together. Justin dressed Sean up like a mannequin and vetoed almost all of Sean's attempts at choosing for himself. Sean had been grateful for the help, even if he grumbled. Justin had an eye for fashion, whereas Sean didn't care what he wore. If his outfit wasn't slightly too big jeans, a T-shirt, and trainers, then it was never at the top of Sean's list. He always dressed for comfort, but Justin helped him do that with a bit of extra style.

Justin gave a put-upon sigh, but he couldn't stop the smile that tugged at the corners of his mouth. The chance to use Sean as a clothes horse and to spend a few hours with him half-naked in a variety of changing rooms? Yeah. No way was Justin going to turn that down. At least it would give him the excuse to legitimately study Sean's arse, albeit through his clothes.

"Yeah. I suppose we could go tomorrow night. It'll be hell though, late-night shopping in the run-up to Christmas. You'll owe me big time."

"I'll pay you in pumpkin spice latte."

"You know me so well." Justin let the grin he'd been trying to suppress escape. "Okay, done. Meet me at Starbucks on Kensington High Street after work, and you can pay me in advance. I'll need all the caffeine and sugar to get me through shopping at the end of my work week."

CHAPTER FOUR

Sean wove his way through the crowds of shoppers. As Justin had predicted, it was manic. Christmas displays adorned every window and the decorations lighting the streets looked as though they were using half the power from the national grid. It was beautiful, but hard to appreciate when you were surrounded by stressed people laden down with carrier bags.

Starbucks was packed, of course, but Sean got there deliberately early. He ordered his coffee in a takeaway cup — just in case — but stood, sipping slowly and watching the occupied tables like a hawk. Finally his patience was rewarded. He spotted a couple of women beginning to gather up their shopping bags, and as soon as one of them pushed their chair back to stand, he made his move.

"Sorry to swoop like a total vulture, but are you leaving?" He gave the woman his most charming smile.

"Oh, um, yes." She smiled back, looking a little dazzled.

Sean was used to that reaction from women. "Mind if I dive in?" He gestured to the table.

"Oh no, of course not. Help yourself."

"Thanks." He waited until they'd gathered up their stuff, and then took the table they'd vacated. While he was waiting, he got out his phone and scrolled through his emails. There was nothing new of interest — just the usual junk or marketing emails, which he quickly deleted.

The sound of a child laughing in delight made him look up. A little boy was giggling at the man opposite him. The man—his dad, Sean assumed—had a splodge of whipped cream on the end of his nose.

"I want one too," the boy said.

His dad dipped his finger in the cream on top of his coffee and dotted it on the boy's nose. The child giggled again.

Sean was amused at their antics, but an ache spread in his chest. He thought back to his own childhood. It was so many years since he'd had a fun, easy relationship with his father—almost too long ago to remember. He knew they'd played football in the park together. Sean had a vague sense of sunshine and smiles, and of feeling happy. But when his mum died when he was eleven, everything had changed. His dad had become withdrawn and distant when Sean had needed him most. That was when Justin's family had become a substitute for Sean's own. Justin's mum, Liz, had minded him every day after school. As Sean's dad worked increasingly long hours, retreating into his job as a way of holding the rest of the world at bay, Sean spent more and more time with Justin and his family. It was easy there, and there was love and laughter, unlike in his own home.

Sean stared at the phone in his hand, considering sending a message to his dad. He hadn't been in contact with him for weeks. His dad didn't even know he was back in the country. Sean knew he ought to get in touch, maybe go back to spend Christmas with him. But he wasn't even sure if he'd be welcome.

He'd put off telling his dad he was gay until a month before he left the country. Sean knew it was a cowardly way to deal with it, but he'd been so afraid of his dad's reaction. It wasn't that he thought his dad would be violent—Sean was bigger than him, anyway—but he couldn't face the inevitable negativity. Sean's dad had made it abundantly clear during his teen years how much he disapproved of Justin.

I don't know why you hang around with that little queer... People will talk, you know... Don't want them to get the wrong idea.

Sean tightened his grip on his coffee cup, the cardboard buckling as he squeezed.

"Hi." Justin's slightly breathless greeting pulled Sean out of his uncomfortable musings. "Sorry I'm late. The Tube was hell on wheels. The first one was so full I couldn't get on, so I had to wait for the next train."

"It's fine."

Justin's pale cheeks were pink from the cold and the tips of his blond hair peeked out of the charcoal beanie he'd pulled low over his ears. He looked adorable. "Sit down. I'll go and get you your coffee."

Sean was back a few minutes later, still empty-handed. "I've ordered, but you need to listen out for your name of the day."

Justin glared at him suspiciously. "Oh God. What did you call me this time?"

Sean grinned. "You'll know it when you hear it."

This was an old joke. Justin started it years ago by ordering their drinks under the name "Dick" and nearly dying from a paroxysm of laughing when the barista yelled it out across the crowded coffee shop. After that they'd run through all other possible rude-sounding names, before branching out into character names from favourite TV programmes, books, and movies.

"Well, whatever it is, I hope they hurry up. I'm desperate for that coffee."

Sean slid his half-empty cup across the table. "It's not pumpkin spice... it's mocha, but you can share while you're waiting."

"Thanks." Justin took the paper cup and cradled it almost reverently in his slender fingers as he took a sip.

Just at that moment, one of the servers yelled out completely deadpan, "Pumpkin spice latte for Draco!"

Justin promptly choked on his mouthful. Face pink, he spluttered and grabbed for a paper napkin that lay on the table.

Sean laughed. "I told you you'd know. Go and get it, then."

He was still chuckling when Justin slid back into his chair with his coffee.

"One of the women waiting for her drink told me I look like him," he said.

"Course you do. That's why it's funny."

"Wanker."

"Come on, Draco's hot."

Justin huffed. But he was too busy scooping whipped cream into his mouth with the stirrer to complain anymore. Sean watched, distracted by Justin's lips and the tip of his tongue as he licked cream from the corner of his mouth.

"What?" Justin had stopped and was looking at Sean inquiringly.

"Nothing." Sean's cheeks heated as he looked away, focusing on the child and his father, who were getting ready to leave. The dad was helping the little boy into gloves and a hat, ready to head out into the chill of the winter evening.

"What are you doing for Christmas this year?" Sean asked Justin.

"Well... I was supposed to be spending it with Andy. But that's obviously off the table now." A shadow of hurt crossed his features, and Sean wished he hadn't asked the question. "So now I'm flying up to see my parents," Justin continued. "I've got time off between Christmas and New Year, so I'm going to Scotland for a few days. Mum's been on at me to visit ever since they moved, and I haven't managed to get up there yet."

Justin's parents had recently relocated to the Scottish Highlands. They'd taken early retirement, bought a place up there, and set up a B & B.

"Nice." Sean tried not to sound wistful. He'd always envied Justin his family. Two loving parents, who accepted him for who he was. He couldn't imagine how that would feel.

"Should be." Justin smiled. "Suzie'll be there too, and I haven't seen her since the summer." Suzie was Justin's older sister.

"Where's she living now?"

"Near Manchester." Justin took a sip of the coffee he'd finally unearthed from beneath its mound of cream. "How about you? You got plans?"

Sean shrugged. Carefully avoiding Justin's gaze, he kept his voice light. "Not sure. I guess I'll go and see my dad." He didn't use the word "home." It hadn't felt like home for a long time, not even while he was still living there.

"Yeah?" Justin's sympathetic tone told Sean he knew exactly how Sean felt about it.

Sean didn't want to have this conversation. He picked up his cup and drained what was left in it. "Come on, drink up. We've got shopping to do."

The shops were mayhem. Sean stayed close to Justin, who swept ahead of him like a man on a mission.

"We're doing your interview clothes first," Justin informed him.

Justin took clothes off racks, and Sean obediently offered his arms to carry the stuff he picked out. He didn't bother to make any suggestions. Experience had taught him that he was better off keeping quiet and letting Justin get on with it.

Once Sean was weighed down with several suits, ties, and shirts, Justin jerked his head towards the changing rooms. "Let's go dress you up."

A cute male shop assistant with dyed black hair checked how many garments they had with them and gave Justin a token. "There's a cubicle free at the far end. You going in together?" His gaze took them both in, lingering a little too long for a straight boy.

"Yes. He can't be trusted to make his own fashion decisions," Justin said.

"My boyfriend's the same," the shop assistant said with a smile.

"We're not—" Sean began, but Justin cut him off smoothly.

"Good thing they have us then, isn't it?" Justin grinned at the guy and patted Sean on the arse, making him jump. "Come on, babe."

"What the hell was that?" Sean asked as Justin whisked the curtain closed behind them.

"That was us practising for tomorrow night. You're going to be my boyfriend, remember? I thought it might be good to get into character early."

That sounded dangerous. Sean wondered what Justin had in mind.

Justin lifted the pile of clothes out of Sean's arms and started hanging them on the hooks on the wall. "Now strip."

Sean stripped obediently. There wasn't really enough room for two men in the tiny cubicle, and as he bent over to ease his jeans off his feet, his arse bumped against Justin. "Sorry," he muttered.

He straightened up, nipples tightening in the cool air. Justin raked his gaze over Sean assessingly. Sean found himself tensing his abs—which was ridiculous; his stomach was pretty flat at the best of times.

"Try these first." Justin held out a pair of charcoal suit trousers and a greyish-purple shirt.

Sean wasn't convinced by the shirt, but what did he know? He put them on.

"And put this tie on too." The tie was silver and a slightly different shade of purple in a diamond pattern.

Finally, Justin helped Sean into the suit jacket.

Sean stared at his reflection. He looked pretty good. Justin stood behind him. He lifted the jacket to examine the cut of the trousers over his arse.

"They're a good fit on you." Justin smoothed a hand over the curve of one of Sean's buttocks, and Sean bit back a sound of surprise. His dick tingled with interest, and he locked that down fast. "The shirt and tie look good too."

"So, is this a keeper?" Sean asked.

"Slow down there," Justin said. "We can't make rash decisions until you've tried on more combinations. Keep these trousers on, but try some of the other shirts first."

Sean was relieved that he got to keep the trousers on for a while. He was pretty sure he was sporting a semi just from that touch of Justin's hand on his arse. This shopping trip was clearly going to be an exercise in self-control.

By the time he was instructed to change his lower half, Sean had managed to calm down enough not to embarrass himself. Once he'd tried on all possible combinations of shirts, suits, and ties, he was hot, bothered, and losing the will to live, which was a pretty effective bonerkiller.

After all that, Justin ended up deciding on the first suit but with a blue rather than a purple shirt, although he'd made Sean try on each of them three times before he made the final decision. Sean gritted his teeth and tried not to bitch. He knew he should be grateful for the help, but *seriously*? How important was it to get exactly the right shade of shirt for his skin tone? Was it really going to give him an edge in an interview?

He was grateful, though, that Justin had brought him somewhere relatively cheap. His budget was minimal, but the whole outfit didn't set him back too badly. He still had some left to spend on party clothes, and hopefully enough for some casual stuff too.

Sean lost count of how many more shops they visited, but it felt like they'd been to every men's clothes shop on Kensington High Street by the time

Justin finally found a combination he was happy with for the party.

He'd put Sean in some slim-fitting grey trousers they'd bought in another shop, and was making him try on a few different shirts with them. The air con was turned up high in these changing rooms, and while Sean was grateful not to be hot and sweaty, he shivered as the chilly air touched his skin.

"That one's a bit thin." Justin grazed Sean's tight nipple with a fingertip through the shirt, making him jerk back. "Unless we're going for the slutty look, and we're not."

"Oi. Handsy."

Justin grinned. "Better get used to it before tomorrow. Andy knows I like PDAs, so he'll be expecting us to be a bit touchy-feely."

The thought of being allowed to touch Justin like a boyfriend sent a thrill through Sean. He wondered what it would involve. Handholding? A few casual touches? Whatever it was, it wouldn't be enough.

He stripped out of the offending shirt. "What's next?"

Justin handed him a dark red one instead. It had a slight sheen to it, only noticeable when it caught the light, and subtle polka dots that were part of the weave rather than in a different colour.

"It's a bit bright, isn't it?"

"It's Christmassy. And you can get away with colours like that with your dark hair, especially with that tan. It'll look good on you."

Sean stared at his reflection for what felt like the millionth time that evening. Dark hair in need of a cut, dark eyes, stubble on his jaw. He looked like a pirate. "I like this one."

He caught Justin's grey gaze in the mirror where he stood behind Sean. Justin slid his hands over Sean's shoulders, the warmth of them heating Sean's skin even through the fabric. He frowned thoughtfully and Sean waited for the verdict.

"Yes. We have a winner."

Sean gave a mental fist pump. Now all he needed was a decent pair of hole-free jeans and a couple of long-sleeved T-shirts.

Final destination was Gap, where somehow Justin talked Sean into trying on a pair of super skinny jeans even though there was no way Sean was going to buy them.

"I hate skinny jeans," he grumbled as he forced his feet through the stupid tight legs and wriggled into them. "They look good on you, but I feel ridiculous in them. And they're way too tight, and it feels weird."

"But they make your arse look seriously good."

Sean could see Justin's gaze fixed on the arse in question. Then Justin's hands were on him again, just a quick squeeze of his arse like a grocery shopper testing fruit for ripeness. Justin's casual examination made Sean feel hot all over.

Justin peered over Sean's shoulder to look at him in the mirror and lifted the front of his T-shirt a little. "Your junk looks good in them too."

The wave of heat that flooded Sean centred on his groin. And oh—there definitely wasn't enough room in these for his dick to do *that*. Okay, maybe there was, but not without it being embarrassingly obvious. He tugged his T-shirt down to hide the rapidly expanding bulge in the front of the jeans that left absolutely nothing to the imagination.

"I don't care," Sean said. "I'm going to get straight-leg ones like I always wear. These make me look like I should be in a boy band."

"Okay." Justin sighed, staring at Sean's arse again, and seriously, he needed to stop. Wasn't he still supposed to be pining over Andy? "Get them off, then. And if the straight-leg ones fit, we can go and get some food and then head home."

"Good idea. I'm starving."

Sean turned his back on Justin so he could hide the tent in his boxers while he dropped trou for the umpteenth time that night. But the stupid skinny jeans got stuck on his feet, and as he was trying to kick out of them, he lost his balance and stumbled back into Justin, who grabbed his hips in a way that didn't help the whole boner situation at all.

"Whoa! Careful."

"My feet are stuck. This is reason 265 why skinny jeans are a fucking stupid invention." Sean sat down on the tiny little bench at the side of the cubicle and hunched over, trying to hide his lap while he started to work the stretchy denim over his too-thick socks. The jeans had turned themselves inside out on the way off and were now doing a great impression of a straightjacket for his legs.

"Let me help." Justin dropped to his knees. He lifted Sean's feet one at a time and eased the jeans off. "Honestly. I think you should be old enough to undress yourself by now."

Although he was helping with the jeans, this whole situation was the exact opposite of helpful for Sean's other predicament. Surely the embarrassment of having his best mate's face a few inches away from his raging erection should have killed his arousal, but it only seemed to ramp it higher in some weird spiral of awkward, shameful hotness. Any minute now, Justin was going to notice. How could he not?

Justin peeled off the offending denim, his attention thankfully focused on the task in hand. When he was done, he sat back on his heels and raked his gaze up Sean's legs—and then got stuck on Sean's crotch. His eyes widened, and Sean watched a pink flush creep over Justin's cheeks as his lips softened into an O of surprise.

Justin seemed to take forever to drag his gaze from Sean's dick to his face, and his grey eyes were darker than usual when they finally met Sean's. But maybe it was due to the light in here. This cubicle was dimmer than some of the others they'd been in this evening.

"Sorry," Sean muttered. "It's nothing personal. But you keep groping me... and it's confusing my dick."

"You're so easy." Justin's voice was teasing, but he sounded a little hoarse, and when he swallowed, the *click* of his throat was audible in the cramped space.

The moment hung there between them, thick with tension. Possibilities lurked at the edges of Sean's consciousness, whispering what-ifs. It would be so easy to start something with Justin there between his knees, to touch his cheek, to lean forward and kiss him, to admit that his arousal *was* Justin-specific and not just about random touch.

But Justin moved before Sean had time to act on any of those impulses. He pushed himself briskly to his feet, his hands gripping Sean's thighs for a brief moment as he used them for leverage.

"Come on, horndog. I'm starving. Let's finish up here and then head somewhere to buy food."

What just happened?

Justin's head tumbled with confusion as he waited outside in the street while Sean was paying. He'd excused himself, claiming he needed a break from the crowds, but really he needed a break from Sean and the weird sexual tension between them. He didn't think he was imagining it. Was there any way Sean might be interested in Justin like that? He'd never shown any sign of it in all the years they'd been friends. But then, he'd kept his sexuality locked down tight for so long, who knew what other secrets he might have hidden?

If Sean fancied Justin, though, surely he would have said something or made a move once he was out? But when Justin thought about it, he realised that he'd almost always been in a relationship with someone else. This was the first time he'd been completely unattached since Sean had come out, apart from before he started seeing Andy, and he'd only been single for a few weeks then….

No.

Justin shook his head to clear his thoughts and stop his stupid imagination taking flight. There was no way Sean could feel the same. An embarrassing erection was hardly a declaration of love. Sean probably hadn't got laid in a while, and Justin had been pretty handsy — he couldn't help himself. It didn't mean anything.

"Hi."

Lost in his thoughts, Justin hadn't noticed Sean emerge from the shop. Laden down with carrier bags, he grinned at Justin, but there was uncertainty there and he still looked sheepish.

"Hey. What do you want to do for dinner? We could cook back at mine, but it's pretty late already. Would you rather eat out?"

A little crease appeared between Sean's brows as he considered this. Then he said, "I think I'm done with the crowds. How about we grab a takeaway from M&S and heat it up at your place."

"Yeah. That sounds good."

The awkwardness between them eased as they wandered the aisles, debating what food to get. Justin wanted Chinese, but Sean said he couldn't face another noodle for at least a month. So they ended up getting pizzas instead, with garlic bread because Justin said Sean needed feeding up, and salad because Justin was — according to Sean — a weird health freak.

"The tomato sauce on the pizza doesn't count as one of your five a day," Justin insisted.

"Well it should, and it's got mushrooms on it too."

"There's about one mushroom on the whole damn pizza. That doesn't count either."

Sean rolled his eyes. "Okay, okay. Get the salad. But I hate eating salad in winter. It's too cold."

Justin chuckled. "We sound like an old married couple. I think we're taking this pretend relationship thing a little far, bickering over our grocery shopping."

Sean smiled, and the warmth in it made Justin's stomach flip. "More practice for tomorrow?"

"Yeah. Nothing like a good domestic to make us look authentic." Justin picked up the bag of salad and put it in the basket he held over one arm. Feeling bold, he took Sean's hand and laced their fingers together. "Is this okay?"

Sean licked his lips and then nodded, a brief jerk of his head. "Sure. I need to get used to touching you before tomorrow, otherwise I'll forget I'm allowed." His palm was warm and his fingers strong when he squeezed Justin's.

The weirdest thing was how it didn't feel weird at all.

Sean kept hold of Justin's hand all the way to the checkout, only letting go when they needed to load their shopping onto the belt.

They didn't hold hands in the street, but they walked close, elbows bumping. Then, on the Tube, they sat with their thighs pressed together. Normally Justin would have tried to put a little space between them, but today he didn't bother. He let himself enjoy the feeling of Sean's leg next to his own and allowed his imagination to run away with a little fantasy about them really being a couple. They were heading home to the flat they shared, ready to eat dinner and then make out on the sofa—

"Isn't this your stop?" Sean nudged Justin and ripped him abruptly from thoughts of being back on his knees in front of Sean again, like earlier but with fewer clothes and more blowjobs.

"Oh bollocks, yes."

They made it off the train just in time.

CHAPTER FIVE

"Hurry up!" Justin banged on the door of his bathroom. They were getting ready to go out to the party and Sean had been in there for ages. "What the fuck are you doing in there? Oh my God. I bet you're wanking in the shower. If you use all the hot water, I'm gonna kill you."

He paced around his bedroom as he waited for Sean to get the hell out so he could have his turn in the bathroom. He'd already laid his clothes out. There was nothing else he could do until he'd showered and washed his hair, and he was way too jittery to sit and chill. The thought of seeing Andy with his new bloke was making him nauseous. Even if he didn't want Andy back, Justin wasn't looking forward to coming face-to-face with his replacement. What did this new guy have that Justin didn't, other than novelty value? Maybe that was all it was. But deep down, Justin couldn't help feeling that he must have done something wrong. Maybe he wasn't good enough in bed, or attractive enough, or interesting enough. He sighed and went to hammer on the door again.

"Come *on*, Sean." At least the water had stopped.

The door opened, and Sean stood there with a towel around his waist, dark hair dripping onto his shoulders. "I still need to brush my teeth, but you can get in the shower if you want."

Justin pushed past him. "I want. We need to leave in forty minutes, and it takes me ages to get my hair right."

He stripped off his clothes, grateful that the air in the bathroom was warm and humid already. Sean was at the sink with his back to Justin, and the mirror was too fogged up for Sean to be able to see a reflection. Justin was glad—he'd always felt skinny and pale next to Sean, and with Sean's current tan, the contrast was even worse than usual. He got into the tub and pulled the shower curtain around him before turning on the water.

He heard Sean say something, but his words were lost against the sound of the shower.

"Huh?" Justin poked his head back through the curtain, to be faced with Sean's bare arse. Sean was using his towel to dry his hair and bending forward as he did it. "Wow. Nice view."

Justin was teasing, but it was true. This angle didn't leave a lot to the imagination. Sean's crack, dusted with dark, soft-looking hairs, led down to his taint, and Justin caught a glimpse of Sean's balls between his legs before he stood up so fast he almost cracked his head on the sink.

"Sorry." As he turned, Sean wrapped the towel around his waist again, but not before Justin had managed to sneak a look at his cock. Soft but plump, and awfully tempting.

"It's okay. I've seen it all before in the locker rooms at school." Although back then, Justin had tried really hard not to look in case anyone noticed. Now, he'd been able to fully appreciate it. His cock throbbed as it thickened and rose, poking into the shower curtain. He moved back a little so Sean wouldn't be able to see it. "What did you say anyway? I didn't hear."

"I was asking if I should shave?" Sean ran his hand over his stubble.

It was long enough to be almost a beard now, thick and dark and sexy as hell.

"No, leave it. Andy couldn't grow a full beard even though he's over thirty, and he was really self-conscious about it. It will only make you more enviable."

"Okay. I might neaten it up a bit, though. Have you got any shaving foam? I'm out."

"In the cabinet over the sink."

"Cheers."

Justin ducked back behind the curtain. He lathered himself up, willing his cock to calm down, but then it was time to wash down there, and that didn't help matters at all. He couldn't resist giving himself a squeeze because it felt so good, and knowing Sean was on the other side of the thin plastic curtain made him feel extra dirty. Apparently he was into almost-exhibitionism, because his cock got harder in his hand and he gave in to the temptation to stroke in earnest for a moment.

He bit back a groan at the perfect, slick grip. If he really let himself go for it, this wouldn't take long. Sean wouldn't hear him over the shower anyway. Maybe he could—

"Can I borrow some tweezers? I need to sort out this unibrow I'm rocking."

Sean's voice was close. *Fuck*, he might be right outside the curtain. Justin snatched his hand away from his dick as though it had burned him, feeling like a right perv.

"Um... I think so." His voice came out embarrassingly high and strained.

"You think so? Helpful, Justin."

"I mean yeah. They're in the cabinet too. Front left."

Okay. I really can't. Justin reluctantly let go of his erection to focus on washing his hair instead, but his body didn't give up on the idea even if common sense did. When he finally heard Sean call "Right, I'll leave you to it," he barely waited for the sound of the bathroom door closing before he took his shaft in hand again and jerked himself to a ridiculously fast climax, with images of Sean's bare arse stuck on replay in his head.

It made a nice change from having sad wanks over the memory of Andy.

"Are we getting the Tube?" Sean asked.

They were almost ready. Justin was putting the finishing touches to his hair. The butterflies in his stomach were back in force now, his post-orgasm high all too quickly blitzed away by nervous tension.

"No. I booked us a taxi." Justin picked up his phone and checked the time. "Fuck! It'll be here in five." He finger-combed his fine blond hair into place. Long on top, but short at the back and sides, the fringe swept sideways across his brow. His narrow face looked back at him from the mirror, tight with tension.

Sean stepped up behind him and put his hands on Justin's shoulders. A steady weight, grounding him. "You look great." His voice was calm and reassuring, with no trace of teasing. "Honestly, Justin. You look gorgeous."

"Yeah?" Justin caught Sean's gaze in the mirror and gave him a small smile.

"Yeah. Andy will wonder why the hell he was stupid enough to let you go."

Justin's smile widened. "You think?"

"I know."

"You look good too." Justin mentally congratulated himself again on the outfit choice. Those trousers showed off Sean's long legs and slim hips beautifully, and the red shirt was a great colour on him. Justin had carefully coordinated his own outfit so they looked good together, his trousers in a slightly paler shade of grey and a purple shirt that blended with Sean's deep red one. Neither of them was wearing a tie, to fit the smart-casual dress code, and Justin had instructed Sean to roll up his sleeves once he'd ditched his jacket. Sean had lovely forearms; it made sense to show them off. "I think we'll turn a few heads when you walk in on my arm." A car horn sounded on the street outside. "That'll probably be the taxi."

"Let's go then, boyfriend. Show Andy what he's missing out on." Sean took Justin's hand, and Justin's heart surged at the contact.

It's only pretend, he reminded himself. But his body hadn't got the memo. The fluttering in his stomach was now for a totally different reason.

As the taxi drove through the busy London streets, away from the residential area where Justin lived and towards the centre, the streets got wider and brighter. Justin's stomach lurched with nerves again.

"Is this a really stupid idea?" he asked. "We don't have to do this if you don't want. We can tell people you're a mate, or we could just duck out of the party altogether and go to the pub, or out for dinner or something."

"Don't be daft." Sean squeezed Justin's hand, which he'd kept hold of throughout the ten-minute cab drive. "We're nearly there now, let's run with it. What could possibly go wrong?"

Justin could think of a few things. Mostly involving dancing, and embarrassing boners, and accidentally rubbing them up against the guy he'd been best friends with since he was seven years old.

He kept his worries to himself. Instead he said, "Maybe we should have discussed limits."

"What do you mean?"

"Like… how far we're prepared to go. I don't want things to be weird." Although Justin had a sneaking suspicion that they were already in weird territory. Sean was still holding his hand and stroking small, distracting circles on the palm with his thumb. It was robbing Justin of the ability to think straight.

"I'm pretending to be your boyfriend in a public place," Sean said. "Unless it's a very different party to the kind of thing I'm imagining, I think we'll be okay. A bit of handholding, casual touches, maybe a kiss on the cheek? I think we can handle that."

Justin's brain got stuck on the word "kiss." On the cheek…. He could do that, but even thinking about it made him imagine more. He'd spent most of his teenage years longing to kiss Sean. Wondering how it would feel, how he'd taste. *God*. He needed to stop thinking like this or he'd get hard again.

"I suppose… but I don't want to put you in an awkward position. Just don't do anything you don't want to do."

"It's okay. We've got a safeword. If I yell 'gibbon,' you'll know we've gone too far."

Justin burst into a surprised snort of laughter. "Okay. Well, that will definitely get us noticed."

Sean grinned, teeth gleaming in the flash of a car headlight from outside. "I think we're there."

The cab was pulling up outside the front of the hotel where the party was being held. Justin let go of Sean's hand to pay the driver. Meanwhile, Sean got out and walked around to open Justin's door.

"Thanks." Justin took Sean's proffered hand and climbed out of the taxi.

Sean laced their fingers together and squeezed. "We've got this."

CHAPTER SIX

They'd aimed to arrive fashionably late, because Justin wanted to make an entrance. But when he saw how packed it was through the double doors that led into the function room, Justin wished they'd got there a little earlier.

Gripping Sean's hand so tightly it was probably painful, Justin pasted a social smile on his face as they walked into the crowded room. His eyes scanned the people until they landed on the person he hoped was paying attention.

Andy was standing off to the side, deep in conversation. His dark head with its short, conservative cut turned towards the man beside him. Andy's companion laughed at something he'd said. Justin gave him a quick once-over. A little taller than Justin, with brown hair and broad shoulders, he was cute, Justin supposed. The jealousy he'd been expecting was more of a flicker than a flare.

As though he could feel Justin looking at him, Andy's new man looked up and met Justin's gaze for a moment. Justin held his head high and drew Sean closer into his side. "There they are," he muttered, still trying to smile and look relaxed. "Has Andy noticed us yet?"

Sean slipped an arm around his waist. "Yep. He just clocked you."

Justin looked back at his ex. He caught the surprise on Andy's face before his ex schooled his features into indifference. He gave Justin a curt nod, which Justin returned.

"He's such a git," Justin muttered. "Can't even manage a smile for the bloke whose arse he used to plough. That's just rude."

Sean stiffened beside him and put a proprietary hand in the small of Justin's back, steering him towards a table where there were trays of drinks laid out waiting. "Come on. I need some alcohol for this."

"Beer goggles, huh? Charming. I'm not that ugly."

"Not for *that*. For this whole situation. Being sociable with people I don't know, dancing later…. You know I can't dance unless I've had a few."

Sean picked up two flute glasses of fizzy stuff and handed one to Justin. "Cheers, darling." His eyes glinted as he grinned and clinked Justin's glass with his own. "It's a pleasure being your plus-one. But I'm not a cheap date, just so you know."

"Do you put out?" Justin deadpanned.

"You'll have to wait and see."

That teasing glint in Sean's eye was still there, and Justin had no clue what was going through his head. Was this all just a joke to him? Was Justin imagining the sexual tension that seemed to be hovering between them, getting thicker by the second? Maybe it was one-sided and Sean was immune.

Suddenly alcohol seemed like a great idea. It might switch off his brain for a while so he could chill and try to enjoy the party. Justin knocked back the stuff in his glass.

"Easy, tiger. I don't think it's supposed to be a shot," Sean said.

"Whatever. There's plenty more where that came from." Justin took a quick look around to check nobody was paying attention and surreptitiously switched his empty glass for a full one.

"Well, if that's the way it is…." Sean downed his too.

"Oh look, there's Jess." Justin caught sight of his friend waving from a table. "Looks like she's saved us some seats."

They made their way over to where Jess was sitting with Kieran and a couple of the other younger employees from their department.

Kieran gave Justin a bright smile, but it dimmed a little when he noticed Sean beside him.

"Hi," Justin greeted his co-workers. "This is Sean. Sean this is Jess, Kieran, Meera, James, and Theresa."

A couple of them had partners with them, so there were more introductions and names that Justin didn't manage to commit to memory. They took the spare seats that Jess had saved for them. Justin was glad she'd kept two next to each other. That would make their mission much easier to accomplish.

"So," Jess said loudly. "This is your new mystery man. It's nice to meet you, Sean. I've heard so much about you."

Sean glanced sidelong at Justin. "Oh, really?"

"Don't worry, Justin only told me good things." She beamed at them both from across the table and gave Justin a wink she probably thought was subtle. But after two glasses of whatever had been provided free on arrival, it really wasn't.

"Well, that's a relief." Sean put his hand on Justin's where it lay on the table.

"Yeah. I've never seen him so goofy over anyone," Jess continued. "It's *so* romantic that you two were friends for so long and then it suddenly turned into more. It must be amazing falling for your best friend."

She was laying it on really thick, but the others seemed to be lapping it up. The other women were listening fondly, the straight guys were looking slightly uncomfortable, and poor Kieran looked as though he might cry. Justin felt a pang of guilt, but he wasn't interested in Kieran anyway, so it was probably for the best that Kieran thought Justin was madly in love with Sean. It would be like ripping off a Band-Aid.

"It is," Justin smiled at Sean. "It makes all those years I spent pining over him as a teenager totally worth it."

Sean tightened his fingers on Justin's hand, and something flitted through his eyes that looked like recognition, or regret. But it was gone before Justin could be sure what it meant. *Did he know?*

"And you never knew I felt the same," Sean said.

Justin's heart skipped a beat and then started up again at what felt like double time. He stared at Sean, searching those dark eyes for a hint of teasing, a reminder that he was playing a part. But all he could see was sincerity. Sean was way too good at this.

"Oh my God!" Jess brought up a hand to cover her heart. "That's so adorable. Well, better late than never, I suppose."

"Absolutely." Justin somehow managed to get the word out. "I'll drink to that." He raised his glass. More alcohol was definitely required.

Once he'd finished what was in his glass, he offered to go to the bar. "Anyone else want anything?"

Some of the others were still sipping at the fizzy stuff, but Jess requested a vodka and tonic and Kieran asked for a pint of lager.

"And what do you want, babe?" Justin asked Sean.

"Lager for me too, but I'll come and help you carry them."

As they approached the bar, they met Andy and his partner leaving it, carrying drinks in their hands. Justin squared his shoulders. With Sean by his side and a couple of glasses of wine inside him, he was ready for the confrontation.

Andy glanced their way but made no effort to greet them. But Justin wasn't going to let him pass without comment.

"Hi, Andy." Justin kept his voice smooth and passive-aggressively polite. "How are you?"

Andy looked surprised to have such a civil greeting from Justin. The last time they'd spoken had been a muttered exchange about a project when communication had been unavoidable. Apart from that, Justin had completely blanked him since the day the shit had hit the fan and he finished telling him what a lying, cheating scumbag he was.

"Uh, hi," he replied. "It's good to see you." He was a terrible liar. His gaze slid sideways to take in Sean who stood beside Justin like a rock, tall and looming, and comforting in his solidity. "Um… this is Johnny."

The brown-haired guy beside Andy smiled. "Hi." He had a sweet face, innocent and open, and Justin suddenly felt sorry for him rather than jealous. He had what Justin had thought he wanted, but now he realised with sudden clarity that he'd had a very lucky escape.

"Hi, Johnny." He turned to Andy again. "You remember Sean?" Justin reached for Sean's hand and drew him closer, raising their linked hands so Andy couldn't miss them. "We finally got our shit together."

Andy's brows drew together. "Oh?"

Sean offered Andy his free hand to shake. Andy took it, and from the slight wince he failed to hide, Justin knew Sean had squeezed hard. He bit back the urge to laugh.

"Yeah," Sean cut in smoothly. "We couldn't keep hiding how we felt about each other anymore. I think we knew before I went away travelling, but the timing wasn't right then."

"And, of course, I was dating you then, and I'm not the type to play around." Justin let a hint of ice slip into his tone as the words "unlike some people" went unspoken.

Poor Johnny was frowning in confusion as he tried to make sense of the conversation.

"So... you guys used to be together?" He gestured between Andy and Justin.

"Oh yes. Until just a couple of weeks ago," Justin said.

Johnny turned to Andy. "But we've been seeing each other for two months." His voice rose. "You said we were exclusive!"

Justin winced. He hadn't realised Andy had been seeing Johnny for so long, or that Johnny had been unaware of Justin's existence. But his wince was for Johnny rather than himself. Poor guy, what a shitty way to find out the bloke you were dating was a cheating wanker.

Andy glared at Justin, his face turning dark red with embarrassment, fury, or both. "Don't listen to him, Johnny. He's just a jealous little shit."

Justin ignored him and carried on as though he hadn't spoken, addressing Johnny again. "Apparently that's what he tells all the boys. I'm sorry, really. I assumed you knew he was with someone else when you met him. I didn't mean to drop that on you now, but it's probably better that you know. You weren't the only guy he was fooling around with while he was with me either."

Johnny rounded on Andy. "Is this true?"

"Of course not. He's lying. He was probably the one cheating on me." Andy flashed a glare at Sean. "Look. Can we talk about this later?" He kept his voice low, trying to defuse the situation. They were already attracting the attention of some nearby partygoers. Justin had a feeling they were waiting for someone to start throwing drinks. He reckoned now was a good time to get away, just in case.

"Well, clearly you two have lots to talk about. We need to go to the bar. Catch you later." Justin tugged on Sean's hand to get him moving.

Both Andy and Johnny ignored them, busy arguing in hushed tones with lots of irate hand gestures.

Justin held in his amusement until they were safely away, and then he collapsed against the bar half-laughing, half-horrified. "Oh my God, did you see his face? But poor Johnny. I feel bad for him."

Sean was chuckling too. "Oh yeah, that was way too much fun. I know what you mean about Johnny, though, but at least he knows what he's dealing with now. If he's got any sense, he'll get out fast." He glanced back to where they were still arguing, in time to see Johnny turn away with an unmistakable "Fuck off," and stalk away into the crowds. "I think maybe he just did."

Back at their table, Justin filled Jess in on the gossip. Kieran listened with interest, but the other people at the table were having their own conversation, not really paying attention to the drama.

"Serves him bloody well right," Jess said emphatically. "Maybe it'll teach him a lesson."

"So, what happened to the other bloke — Johnny? Is he still here, or did he leave?" Kieran asked.

Justin scanned the room until he caught sight of a man standing alone at the bar, his golden brown hair was the right colour, but he had his back to them, head down, phone in hand. "I think that might be him at the bar." The man in question lifted his head and turned enough so Justin could see his profile. "Yeah, that's him."

"He's cute," Kieran said.

"He is," Sean agreed.

Justin felt a rush of jealousy, which reminded him that they were supposed to be boyfriends — if only for the night. Maybe this was how method actors felt.

"Oi." He nudged Sean with his knee.

"Not as cute as you, obviously." Sean put his hand on Justin's thigh and squeezed, then left it there. It was way too close to Justin's crotch to be a platonic gesture, and Justin felt a delicious tickle of arousal at the warm weight of it.

"He seemed like a decent bloke," Justin said to Kieran. "And he could probably use some company right now. He's having a shitty night."

Kieran's eyes lit up. "You reckon?"

"Go for it."

"Okay." Kieran stood, squaring his shoulders as if he were heading into battle. "I will."

"Good luck," Justin called after him. Then he turned back to Sean and Jess. "I really need to see Andy's face if Kieran manages to pull Johnny right under his nose."

"Is Andy still here?" Jess asked. "God, after a scene like that, I'd be out of here."

"Oh, he's way too brazen to leave. Plus he has arse-kissing to do. He's hoping for a promotion after Christmas, so he's not going to miss a chance to schmooze up to senior management. Look" — Justin pointed — "there he is talking to the head of HR right now. What a surprise. It's a shame Johnny didn't pour a drink over him. That would have sent him home."

Sean patted Justin's thigh, sending another curl of heat to his groin. "But if he'd gone home, he wouldn't get to see us snogging on the dance floor later. We don't want him to miss that. It's another chance to rub his nose in it."

There was going to be snogging? Justin didn't remember agreeing to that. Not that he was opposed to it, but…. Justin's brain short-circuited for a moment, trapped between the thought of kissing Sean and the sensation of Sean's hand idly stroking his thigh. He was glad the table was hiding his lap, because he was pretty sure he'd have a noticeable bulge in his trousers by now.

By the time the food was brought out, Justin had calmed down enough that he could walk across the room to the buffet without embarrassing himself. He was also feeling pretty buzzed from the beer on top of the drinks they'd had when they arrived. Some food seemed like a good idea to soak it up.

They loaded their plates and took them back to the table.

"These breaded chicken strips are lush," Sean said enthusiastically.

"Oh. I didn't get any of those."

"Here, have one of mine." Sean put one on Justin's plate.

"Thanks. And you should try this quiche — it's really good." He was already holding it in his hand, so he offered it to Sean to take a bite.

"Mmmm." Sean nodded as he chewed. "Yeah, that's nice too."

"You've got crumbs on your face." A few bits of pastry had flaked off and attached themselves to Sean's stubble. "No, the other side." Justin reached up and brushed them off carefully. Sean's chin was rough against his fingertips and made Justin imagine how it would feel under his lips. "There."

"Thanks." Sean's smile was soft and weirdly intimate. Justin lost himself in it for a moment, smiling back.

Jess leaned over the table conspiratorially. "God, you two are really good at this. If I didn't know better, I'd swear you were totally in love. It's so sweet it's almost nauseating. Maybe you should reconsider an alternative career in acting."

Justin snapped back to reality. "Yeah, well." A flush warmed his cheeks. "I was pretty good in the drama productions at school, if I say so myself."

This was the easiest role he'd ever had to play. He hadn't even been consciously trying. It felt totally natural to touch Sean like that, to look him in the eyes and smile as if nobody else in the room was watching.

He glanced sideways, trying to check Sean's reaction to what Jess had said, but Sean had his head down, concentrating on his food again. His cheeks looked a little pink too… maybe it was just because it was hot in here.

Once the meal was over, the lights dimmed and the music went up a few notches. People started to drift onto the dance floor.

"Come on," Jess said to the table at large. "Let's dance. I need to work off all the chocolate fudge cake I ate. I love this track, but I'm not going up there on my own."

She managed to rally a bit of support, and as some of the others stood to join her, Sean raised his eyebrows at Justin.

"You wanna?"

Justin raised his eyebrows in return. "Are you sure you've drunk enough?"

Sean mock glared. "Ha-ha. I think I'll manage. It's nice and crowded, and the lights are low."

They found a bit of space on the floor and danced as a group, gradually drifting closer to the DJ.

Justin watched Sean as he moved. Sean was way better at this than he thought he was. He had rhythm, and when he stopped being self-conscious and let the music lead him, he looked loose and natural as he swayed to the beat. The music was upbeat and fast, a mix of modern tracks with plenty of seventies disco thrown in. Nobody was dancing as a couple yet, so Justin had no physical contact with him, but he found it hard to look away. He kept catching Sean watching him too, and they'd smile at each other, or laugh at each other's deliberately cheesy disco moves.

They danced for ages, the group growing and shrinking around them as people came and went. Other colleagues joined them for a while before drifting off to the bar, or for a breather. Justin was getting high on it. He loved dancing, loved moving his body and losing himself in the pure physical pleasure of it. It was like sex—you had to turn off your thinking head and let yourself be carried along on the rush of endorphins as your body took over.

The music changed suddenly as the lights dimmed further. Sliding into a slower, more sensual beat with deep bass tones that vibrated through Justin with the thud of his heart. Without thinking too much about what he was doing, he reached for Sean, who moved towards him willingly. Their bodies slotted together as though they were made for this. Hands found waists and slid around necks, pulling each other close until they were like one, moving to the dirty, sexy rhythm that grabbed Justin like a fist around his cock.

CHAPTER SEVEN

Sean felt as though he was drowning. Swept away on a rising tide of desire, reality and imagination merged, and he struggled to remember this wasn't real. Justin wasn't really his... but Justin's hot breath skimmed Sean's neck, and Sean slipped further into the fantasy. Justin smelled so good, his scent breaking through the overlay of cologne and hair product. Warm and delicious, Sean couldn't get enough of him. Having Justin in his arms was intoxicating, devastating. Everything Sean had wanted for years was finally right there for the taking.

It's only pretend.

Sean pulled away, trying to find air to breathe that wasn't full of Justin. Maybe then he could clear his senses and convince his libido to stand down. But Justin curled his hand into the hair at the nape of Sean's neck and kept him there.

"Stay," Justin said into Sean's ear, making him shiver. "Andy's watching us."

The reminder of why they were doing this should have been a bucket of cold water for Sean, but logic and reason were long gone. Instead he found himself saying, "Well then, let's really give him something to see."

He drew back enough that he could see Justin's face as he brought a hand up to cup his cheek. Justin's lips parted and his eyes glittered in the flashing lights.

"Can I?" Sean asked, hoping Justin could read the meaning even if he couldn't hear the words.

He got a nod in reply, and Justin licked his lips, making them shine, wet and inviting.

So Sean kissed him.

They were both tentative at first. Gentle and almost chaste, soft lips and closed mouths. But then they bumped noses and that made them both smile. Feeling bolder, Sean kissed Justin harder, and when their tongues touched, it was electric. Sean's senses lit up like a Christmas tree when the fairy lights go on, and everything was bright and beautiful. His heart swelled, pounding in his ears and stealing his breath. They were still moving together, but whether it was to the pulsing rhythm of the music or that of their own bodies in response to the heat surging between them, Sean couldn't tell.

He knew they should stop. This kiss was too dirty for an office party, even in the semidarkness of the dance floor, and if he didn't pull away soon, he wasn't sure he'd be able to. If he'd wanted Justin before he'd kissed him, it had been a pale shadow of desire to the burning need he felt now he had Justin in his arms, mouth open and wet, cock grinding hard against Sean's hip.

He broke the kiss, but Justin chased his mouth, hand still in Sean's hair, pulling almost painfully as he tried to keep Sean where he wanted him.

Sean moved his mouth to Justin's ear, where he'd be sure Justin would hear him. "Gibbon." He added an apologetic kiss to Justin's cheek.

Justin burst out laughing and released his grip on Sean's hair, letting his hand slide down to his shoulder as he drew back and put some space between them. "I can't believe you just said that."

"It was that or risk coming in my new trousers." His arousal must have been obvious, so there seemed little point in being coy. Justin was hard too.

There was a flare of heat in Justin's eyes, and then a long pause before he asked, "Do you want to get out of here?"

Did that mean what Sean hoped it meant? "Yeah," he said with a nod, and Justin's smile widened.

"Come on, let's go home." Justin took Sean's hand and led him off the dance floor.

"Look." Sean nudged Justin, attracting his attention to where Kieran and Johnny were dancing, bodies close and hands wandering.

As Justin watched, they started kissing. "Aw, that's sweet," he said. "I'm glad Johnny's night didn't turn out too badly after all."

"Andy doesn't look too happy about it."

Justin followed Sean's gaze to Andy, who was standing at the bar with a drink in his hand and a scowl on his face. "Good."

As they picked up their jackets from the table and made their excuses, Jess gave them a knowing look.

"Sean's still jet-lagged," Justin said smoothly. "I need to get him into bed."

Jess snorted. "I bet you do."

Sean's cheeks flushed hot, but Justin looked totally unfazed. "Is Andy watching us?" He asked Jess, who was sitting facing the room.

She glanced quickly over his shoulder. "Yep."

Justin grinned. "Awesome. Come on then, baby. Let's make our exit. Put your arm around me, and grope my arse on the way out."

In the taxi they stayed sitting close together.

Sean wanted to ask what they were doing, but he was afraid of breaking the spell they'd woven through their pretence, which had conjured something real yet all too tenuous. Delicious anticipation pooled in his belly. He was still hard, hoping that Justin's mind was in the same place his was. He put his hand on Justin's thigh again, feeling taut muscle there. Sean stroked tentatively, watching Justin for any reaction. Justin licked his lips, but kept his gaze fixed out of the window.

Sean slid his hand a little higher, deliberately letting his little finger brush against the bulge at Justin's crotch. Justin glanced at Sean then, just for a second before looking away again. Without saying a word, he covered Sean's hand with his own.

Sean felt a twist of disappointment, expecting Justin to push his hand away.

Instead, Justin pulled it higher, placing it right over the hard length of his cock where it lay jutting sideways, trapped in his clothes.

Okay, so we're on the same page, then.

Sean looked at the taxi driver, checking he couldn't see where Sean's hand was. Thankfully this guy wasn't the chatty type. There was no way Sean could have carried on a conversation right now. He let his fingers move, carefully exploring the shape of Justin through his trousers. Justin kept absolutely still, eyes still tracking the houses and cars as they drove through the London streets, but when Sean rubbed the head of his cock with a fingertip, Justin bit his lip and swallowed, throat bobbing in the dim light.

Sean shifted in his seat. He adjusted himself with his free hand and felt the warm stickiness of precome in his underwear. His cock ached with the need for stimulation. He was stupid with it, and a few strokes would be enough to bring him off. Thinking about that, he rubbed Justin's cock harder, using his palm to touch as much as he could. He wondered whether Justin could come like this, whether he wanted to.

Then the taxi slowed, and they were back at Justin's flat. He pulled his hand away as the driver turned on the light in the back and twisted around to tell them the fare.

Justin reached into his jacket pocket for his wallet, but Sean beat him to it. He shoved fifteen quid into the driver's hand. "Keep the change." He was already opening the cab door. The need to get Justin inside and alone was a biological imperative.

"Cheers, mate," the driver said as they climbed out. "Have a good night."

They made it indoors with indecent haste. Sean was heartened that Justin seemed in as much of a rush as he was.

As soon as the door to Justin's flat closed behind them, Justin grabbed Sean and kissed him again. This time there was nothing hesitant about it. It was all messy urgency as Justin backed him up against the wall and worked his hand down into Sean's waistband. Sean sucked in his stomach to help him gain access and then moaned as Justin's questing fingertips stroked the sensitive tip of his dick. It was delicious torture, but it wasn't enough.

Sean tugged at his belt, unfastening it, tearing at the button and zip so that Justin could stroke him properly if he wanted, then started work on Justin's trousers too. With their hands busy at each other's crotches, it was an awkward fumble, but somehow they got there. Jackets hanging open, trousers around their knees, they finally got their hands around each other's cocks and stroked frantically as they snogged like teenagers.

Sean had imagined this so many times when they were younger that he couldn't believe it was finally happening. What if this was the only chance he'd ever get? He didn't want this to be over too quickly. He tried to pull away, to slow things down and suggest they move somewhere other than the hallway—

Justin moaned in protest. "Don't stop. I'm so close."

The broken, desperate sound of Justin's voice made Sean's balls tighten. "Fuck, me too... but Justin, wait—"

Too late.

Justin came with a groan, his release slicking Sean's fist as his head dropped to Sean's shoulder and his body shuddered. "I'm sorry," he muttered. "I couldn't stop."

He sounded embarrassed, and Sean didn't want that. "It's fine, really... I'm about to join you." Justin had stilled his hand as he came, and Sean was right there, teetering on the edge. He thrust into Justin's hand as a reminder to move it. "Justin, please. I'm desperate here."

Justin chuckled. "I'm on it."

Sean looked down as Justin started to stroke him again. The sight of Justin's fingers, slender and strong around his cock, the head emerging with each slide of his hand was all it took. Sean came with a stifled curse, shooting between them and making a mess of Justin's shirt.

Sean felt Justin's lips brush his cheek, and he turned his head, seeking another kiss. When they parted, both still breathless, Justin looked down.

"Bloody hell. Look at the state of us," Justin said.

"These clothes are all machine washable, right?" Sean wiped a sticky hand on his shirt. "At least we made it inside the front door."

"That was a fucking miracle in itself. I was seriously tempted to blow you in the taxi." Justin grinned.

Sean smiled back, hopelessly smitten. Yet he was already bracing himself for the weirdness that would soon come barging into this intimate space between them, chasing away the possibility of anything more. "I don't want this to be over," he blurted in a rush of honesty. "That was why I didn't want you to come so fast. I don't know what we're doing, or why, and maybe we can think about that tomorrow. But I want more of this." He gestured between them, heart pounding hard as he waited.

Justin's smile had faded to be replaced by caution, as though he were looking for a catch. "I'm up for more," Justin finally said, and Sean breathed a sigh of relief. "Well—" Justin looked down at his dick, which was mostly soft now. " —I can be in a little while. If we're going to have drunken, bad-decision buddy sex, we might as well do it in style, right? Bedroom?"

They pulled their trousers back up so they could walk there without tripping. But as soon as they were in Justin's room, Justin started shedding his clothes. Sean watched as he stripped, revealing his pale skin and lean, smooth body. When he was down to his socks and underwear, Justin looked up and frowned. "This isn't a free show. Get your kit off."

Justin was naked before Sean had finished his shirt buttons, and he came and batted Sean's hands away. Together they got Sean out of his clothes between kisses.

"Chilly?" Justin asked, rubbing his fingertips over Sean's tight nipples.

"Yeah." Sean shivered, but not entirely from the cold. He was already getting hard again. Justin's skin was so smooth and warm. Sean wanted to kiss him all over.

"Get into bed, I'll go and put the heating on for an hour. I don't want to have to blow you under the covers, or I'll suffocate."

Sean's cock lifted a few more degrees at the thought of Justin's mouth on him. All his teenage fantasies were coming to life right there. He gave up a silent prayer of thanks for the chain of events that had led them to this. Even if it was only for one night.

Sean got under the covers while Justin nipped out to the hallway to fiddle with his thermostat. When he came back, he burrowed under the duvet next to Sean, all cold hands and feet that made Sean squirm. His mouth was warm, though, and when they started kissing, the heat built quickly between them in more ways than one.

"Why have we never done this before?" Justin asked as he moved down to kiss Sean's neck, rubbing his cheek against Sean's stubble like a cat.

"You were always with someone after I came out," Sean reminded him. "Well... apart from before you met Andy. But there were only a few weeks between Conrad and Andy, and I was supposed to be leaving the country soon."

"But you wanted to?"

Sean couldn't see Justin's expression. The question sounded casual, but for Sean it was loaded. "You're pretty easy on the eye. I wouldn't have kicked you out of bed if you'd offered."

"Wow. You really know how to turn on the charm." Justin's teeth closed on Sean's neck and bit a little harder than was fun.

Sean yelped, and Justin licked it instead, maybe as an apology.

"Well, what about you?" Sean asked. "Would you have been into it when we were younger?"

"Um. Hell, yes."

"Well, how come you never said or at least hinted?"

Justin raised his head then. His fair hair fell over his forehead and his grey eyes were almost luminous in the dim light of the lamp by the bed. "I thought you were straight, you idiot. I wasn't going to wreck the best friendship I ever had by coming on to you. Of course I fancied you. You're gorgeous, who wouldn't? Plus I *liked* you. It was more than sexual. I had a ridiculous crush on you for years. But when you came out, I was going out with George."

The raw honesty of his words shone through, and Sean could see the shadow of past hurt in Justin's eyes. It was all a long time ago. He'd used the past tense. Would it make him feel any better now to know that Sean had felt the same, all that time, or would it lace his memories with even more regret for lost opportunity? Sean didn't want to kill the mood of what they had now by getting heavy. So instead of all the things he could have said, he reached down to brush a strand of hair away from Justin's face, his hand lingering by his cheek. "I'm sorry I didn't tell you I was gay sooner."

Justin gave a small smile. "You've already apologised for that."

"It never felt like enough."

Justin's smile turned dirty and a glint of mischief lit up his eyes. "Nothing says I'm sorry like a really amazing blowjob. Just a suggestion."

Sean rolled them over, pinning Justin to the bed and laughing. "You're such a tart."

"Yep." Justin tangled his fingers in Sean's hair and kissed him some more. Then he pushed Sean's head south. "Now get down there and show me how good you are at apologising."

CHAPTER EIGHT

Justin's head spun as Sean's hot breath tickled his belly, soft lips and scratchy stubble teasing his sensitive skin and sending sparks of sensation to his cock.

What had he just admitted? He cursed the alcohol he'd drunk tonight and his stupid mouth for running away with him. Why had he told Sean about his adolescent crush? He didn't want to come across as needy and scare Sean off from whatever was about to happen between them, because he knew that this would probably be a one-off. Even if Sean was interested in more than one night of fun, he wasn't settled in London. He didn't have a permanent job — or even a job at all. Sean could end up living in a different city next month. Justin wanted to take what he could get while it was on offer and not ruin it by trying to make it into more than it was.

He pushed Sean's head lower, needing the distraction of Sean's mouth on his cock. Once that happened, Justin was sure there wouldn't be any room left in his brain for actual thoughts. But Sean seemed determined to torture him, because instead of sucking Justin's dick, he bypassed it and started kissing his thighs instead.

"Oh God, you're such a shit," Justin groaned.

Sean chuckled, the sound muffled where his face was pressed into sensitive skin, and then he turned his attention to Justin's balls. Justin supposed that was at least one step closer to where he really wanted Sean's mouth, so he shut up and let him get on with it. Sean had pushed Justin's thighs wide for access, and Justin tried not to focus on how exposed he felt. It was weird how it was way more intimidating doing this with someone he'd known for so long. He'd never had issues with hooking up in the past, happy to open his legs and offer his arse to anyone he was attracted to. But it felt bizarre having Sean, his oldest friend in the world, getting busy down there between his thighs, seeing Justin in a whole new way.

They'd never talked about sex much. Before Sean came out, Justin had never raised the topic for obvious reasons, but even afterwards they'd never discussed their sex lives. Justin had always assumed Sean didn't bring it up because of his natural reticence — he wasn't an oversharer like Justin. Justin usually liked nothing better than quizzing his friends about the gory details of their sexual encounters, but he hadn't wanted to hear about Sean with other guys, so he'd never asked. He didn't even know whether Sean was a top or a bottom, but he was getting toppy vibes now as Sean pushed Justin's knees towards his chest and his mouth moved lower instead of higher.

"Is this okay?" Sean murmured. "I really want to eat you out."

Justin's cock jerked its appreciation and drooled precome onto his stomach.

"Why does that sound about a million times more dirty coming out of your mouth than it has in any porn I've ever watched?"

"Is that a yes?" Sean's dark gaze flicked up to meet Justin's, before Justin threw his head back onto the pillow, closed his eyes, and let Jesus take the wheel.

"Yes, it's a yes. I guess I can accept an apology rim job in place of the... *ahhhh.*"

Sean's tongue started tracing gentle, tantalising, ever-decreasing circles around the sensitive skin of Justin's hole, and Justin lost the ability to make any sounds other than desperate, needy noises. He should probably feel embarrassed about them, but he was too turned on to give a fuck.

Sean was ridiculously good at this. Either that, or it was luck that his technique meshed perfectly with what Justin liked. Some guys were too aggressive with rimming for Justin. He'd never been a fan of someone trying to get their tongue inside him. Obviously some people probably loved that, but for Justin it was too much. Dicks or fingers on the inside? Yes please. But the squirmy feeling of the tip of a tongue working its way into his hole made his toes curl — and not in the good way. The relentless, slow lap of Sean's tongue was perfect. He used just enough pressure not to tickle, but it was light enough to send delicious tingles of sensation through the triad of Justin's arse, balls, and dick. They were linked together in a feedback loop of arousal, sending him higher and higher with every stroke.

Justin had never come without stimulation on his cock before, apart from during wet dreams as a teenager — coincidentally usually ones about Sean — but tonight he wondered if it might be possible. Part of him wanted to find out, to let Sean carry on with what he was doing until Justin either came all over himself or died of sexual frustration, whichever happened first. He thought about touching himself, but Sean was in charge, and Justin liked him being in the driving seat. The firm grip of Sean's hands on his thighs and the slow measured way he was taking Justin apart pushed all Justin's buttons.

"I need to come," he finally gasped. "Please, Sean."

Sean paused what he was doing to ask, "What do you want?"

"Anything. Just make me come."

Sean knelt up between Justin's legs, his cock jutting out hard and red. Justin wanted it in his mouth so badly—but later. The overwhelming need to come his brains out eclipsed everything else right now. He cried out in delicious ecstasy as Sean closed his fist around Justin's cock in a tight, perfect grip. He reached between Justin's legs with his other hand and circled Justin's hole with his fingers. It was so wet with spit down there that there was no need for lube.

"Oh fuck, yes. Don't stop. That's so good." Justin tensed up, his impending orgasm drawing his muscles tight, like a coiled spring. He dug his heels into the bed, arching, begging with his body as well as his words. When he came, it tore through him, his whole body jerking as he thrust into Sean's hand. Sean's fingers slipped inside, just a little, and Justin clenched around them as his cock pulsed and shot. There wasn't as much spunk this time, but his orgasm was no less powerful for that. Sean drew it out of him, making it last until Justin flopped back on the bed, exhausted, and Sean finally released him.

Sean ran a finger through a smear of come on Justin's belly and then lowered himself over Justin to kiss him again. He straddled Justin with his strong, hairy thighs, and Justin felt the hard nudge of his cock against his own softening one.

He put a hand down and cupped Sean's balls, gently encouraging him to move up the bed. "Here," he said as Sean knee-walked up until his balls bumped Justin's chin. "Let me suck you."

"Do you want me to put on a condom?" Sean asked.

"Do you need to?"

Sean shook his head. "I haven't done anything without one since I got tested last."

"Then I'd prefer to taste you than the latex. And I got myself checked out after Andy."

Justin had been to the clinic after everything fell apart—not that he'd let Andy bareback him anyway, thank fuck, so the risk had been low, but he'd needed to be sure.

He guided Sean's cock into his mouth. The flavour of sex and salt flooded his tongue. Sean was leaking precome liberally. It was good to know that eating Justin out had obviously been good for him too. He tried to take Sean deep, but the angle was all wrong. He sucked on the head for a while, and although Sean seemed to be enjoying that from the sounds he was making, Justin was greedy for more. With a renewed surge of energy, he released Sean and pushed on his hip. "Lie down. I can't deep-throat you like this, and I want to."

Sean moved obediently, lying on his back with one hand behind his head and the other on his belly. He looked so fucking hot laid out on Justin's bed. Justin paused for a moment to admire him.

"What are you waiting for?" Sean took his cock in his hand and stroked it slowly, pulling the foreskin back with each stroke to reveal the shiny, slick head while Justin watched.

"Just looking at you. Appreciating the scenery."

Sean smiled, and his gaze roved over Justin, lingering on his nipples and then drifting down to Justin's soft cock. "Yeah. It's not too shabby from this angle either." He moved his hand back to his stomach, stroking through the soft dark hair there, and his cock flexed expectantly.

Justin crawled over him and kissed him. He owed Sean some teasing, so he took his time working his way down Sean's body again. He buried his face in Sean's neck, breathing in the sweet, earthy scent of his sweat. Then he moved down over Sean's torso, finding his nipples in the crisp chest hair and making them harden under his tongue. Sean wriggled, ticklish, but he settled as Justin licked and sucked his way down to the smooth skin on his hips. His belly was flat and the vee of muscle was taut and defined as he tensed under Justin's mouth.

"God, Justin, I'm dying here," he murmured in a husky voice.

"Nobody ever died from being made to wait to get off." Justin took Sean's cock in a firm grip, lifting it so that Sean would feel his breath as he spoke. He licked his lips, his gaze fixed on Sean's.

"You're evil."

"But you love me anyway," Justin said. Sean's eyes flew wide for a moment, so Justin clarified, "You told me so that time we got drunk on your dad's whisky when we were fourteen. Remember? You said I was your best friend ever and you'd always love me."

"Yeah, I remember." Sean's voice was hoarse and he swallowed hard. For a moment it looked as though he was going to say something else, but nothing came out. Justin stared at him, searching for something in his face that might give him the courage to admit that he loved Sean—not just as a friend—and that he always had. But the shutters had come down over Sean's expression, and Justin was in danger of wrecking the mood unless he got them back on track. A mouth on Sean's cock ought to do it.

"Well, I guess this isn't going to suck itself," Justin said, lowering his head.

Sean's laugh turned into a gasp as Justin took him deep, forcing himself down on Sean until his throat ached and his eyes watered.

"Oh God, Justin." Sean put his hands on Justin's head, his knees coming up to cradle Justin as he sucked in long, slow movements.

He let Sean's cock nudge right into the back of his throat with each pull of his mouth, squeezing around it and making Sean groan before lifting off and using his tongue on the head on each upstroke.

It wasn't long before Sean gasped, "I'm gonna come."

As if Justin would ever pull off. *Fuck that*. Justin had jerked off a hundred times imagining Sean's dick in his mouth. There was no way he was going anywhere until he'd had the full experience. He made an incoherent sound of encouragement, bracing himself for the bitter salt of Sean's come. Even after a few years of doing this on a regular basis, it still sometimes took him by surprise. Come flooded his mouth, and he swallowed as he carried on sucking, pulling out another cry from Sean.

When Justin finally let Sean slip from between his lips, Sean's hands were still in his hair, petting him as he raised his eyes to meet Sean's. Sean smiled, face soft and open now. He looked totally happy and blissed out. Justin's heart skipped a few beats as warmth surged through him.

"C'mere." Sean guided him up with a firm hand at his nape. He licked at Justin's lips. "You taste like me."

Justin shivered. "Well, yeah. I probably missed a bit." He parted his lips and let Sean in, their tongues moving languidly together.

They rolled onto their sides, still kissing, until it gradually slowed to gentle pecks and nuzzling of cheeks. It was so sweet, so perfect, so precisely what Justin had always longed for and never quite found with any of the other guys he'd been with. But maybe that was because none of them had been Sean. He trusted Sean so deeply, with that kind of bone-deep knowledge that someone is on your side whatever happens.

"Can I sleep in here tonight?" Sean asked, sounding half-asleep already. "I'm too tired to move."

"As long as you don't snore," Justin replied. He turned onto his side away from Sean to switch off the lamp. He settled back down on that side, but he pulled Sean's arm over his waist and smiled when Sean snuggled in behind him.

As Sean's breathing slowed into the rhythm of sleep, Justin felt an icy finger of anxiety tapping at the window of his consciousness now the heat of the moment had passed. Would he regret this in the morning? Would Sean? Would things be weird?

Justin sighed. Whatever happened, this night would always be special to him. All he could do was trust that their friendship was strong enough to survive a little awkwardness.

CHAPTER NINE

Sean was the first to wake in the morning. For a moment he couldn't work out where the fuck he was, and why there was a warm, bare body curled around his own naked skin.

Then he remembered.

Fuck... Justin.

Memories of the night before assaulted him, leaving him whirling with mixed emotions. Happiness and excitement were soon overshadowed by worry and... regret? No, not regret. He would never wish that amazing night away, but bloody hell. He hoped they'd be able to get back to normal afterwards, because he really didn't want to have fucked up all those years of friendship for one hedonistic night.

He didn't think Justin would want a repeat, and even if he did, it seemed like a bad idea. Justin was on the rebound from Andy, and that must be influencing any decisions he made at the moment. Guilt rushed through Sean at the thought that he'd taken advantage of Justin when he was vulnerable. Maybe he should have put a stop to things before they'd got out of hand.

His brain was running away with him, and there was no chance of him going back to sleep now. Plus he was desperate for a piss. He rolled carefully out of Justin's arms and tried to get out of the bed without making it rock and creak too much.

Justin stirred and sighed in his sleep, turning over and throwing an arm across the warm space where Sean had lain. His lashes were dark against his cheeks, and the winter sunlight filtering through a gap in the curtains caught his pale hair and turned it to gold. He looked so peaceful and content. Longing spiked through Sean. He wished he could come back to bed with coffee and breakfast for both of them and wake Justin with kisses. But that was what boyfriends did, and they weren't boyfriends. Not now in the cold, wintry light of this December morning. The party was over, and the illusion had faded away, like Cinderella's gown turning back into rags once the magic wore off. Sean flushed at the fanciful thought.

Sighing, Sean found his boxers from the night before and pulled them on. They were a little crusty in places, but he'd get some clean ones later when he could shower without waking Justin. He didn't want to put his party clothes back on, but he was freezing now he'd left the shared warmth of the bed, so he picked up a T-shirt that was lying over the back of Justin's chair and pulled it on. It was a little small, and the scent of Justin made Sean's heart clench.

He crept out, pulling the door gently closed behind him.

In the kitchen he brewed some coffee and then went to sit on the sofa and wrapped himself in a blanket. He put the TV on for distraction but couldn't focus on it. Instead he stared out of the window at the vivid blue of the winter sky. He clutched the hot mug in his hands and sipped at the scalding liquid while he waited for Justin to wake. Then they could talk about what happened last night.

Justin finally emerged an hour or so later.

"Morning." Justin's voice was rough and his usually bright eyes were still puffy from sleep. He was dressed in a T-shirt and some pyjama bottoms that were so threadbare it was obvious he wasn't wearing anything underneath them. Sean's gaze snagged on the movement of Justin's soft bulge as he walked into the room, and he was assaulted by a vivid sense memory of Justin's hard cock in his hand, of Justin arching and straining beneath him, lost to everything but Sean and the way he was touching him.

Heat flashed through Sean as his whole body lit up with wanting more. He tore his eyes away and met Justin's sheepish smile.

"Morning." Sean forced out the reply through a dry throat.

There was a long pause.

"So…." Justin's face was wary. "This is a bit weird, huh?"

"A bit, yeah."

Sean had hooked up with friends before, and it hadn't been a problem. They'd either hooked up again until one of them got bored with it, or they'd laughed it off and gone back to how things were before. But those were friends he fancied a bit or thought were hot. They weren't friends he'd been hopelessly in love with for years. Sean's heart thudded against his ribs as he finally admitted it to himself—this was way beyond physical attraction. He was in love with Justin, and deep down he'd always known it.

"I'm sorry." Justin sat beside Sean on the sofa, avoiding his gaze. He twisted his hands and started cracking his knuckles in sequence, a nervous habit Sean recognised.

"What? Why are you sorry? It took two of us."

"Yeah, but if I hadn't got you to pretend to be my boyfriend—"

"That was my idea."

Justin shrugged. "I suppose. But I think we took the pretending a little far." He cracked another knuckle and Sean winced.

He put his coffee on the table and took Justin's hands, holding them still. He needed to reassure Justin that they were fine. Everything was fine. "It's no big deal. We had fun; don't act like it's a problem. Because for me, it isn't. We're friends. That's the most important thing."

He wasn't sure that was true. He had a suspicion that the emotional fallout from the physical devastation of the night before was going to take a long time to fade. But that was his problem, not Justin's. Justin didn't know how Sean felt, and seeing his discomfort now, Sean was glad he hadn't let his guard down. He didn't want to complicate things further. Their friendship came first.

Justin finally turned to meet Sean's gaze. His grey eyes were hard to read, and there was still a notch of concern etched between his eyebrows that Sean wanted to smooth away with a touch, or a kiss.

"Yeah, it is. I wouldn't want to fuck up our friendship over one mad—but awesome—night." He smiled, tentatively at first, but when Sean smiled back, it widened.

Sean chuckled. "It was pretty awesome."

And then they were both laughing, the tension dissipating like birds taking flight.

"If only we'd known when we were younger, though. All those sleepovers wasted, talking when we could have been...." He didn't finish the sentence.

"Yeah," Sean agreed.
If only.

Justin swallowed down the disappointment that lay on his chest as a heavy, crushing weight. He was relieved that the awkward morning-after conversation was over, but the outcome wasn't what he'd been hoping for. He cursed himself for being too chicken to be honest with Sean and admit that he'd have liked more than a one-off. To Sean it might be no big deal, but it was a fucking huge deal to Justin.

His teenage crush was out in the open now, but he hadn't admitted to Sean it had grown stronger over the years, putting down roots and spreading branches instead of fading and withering away like he'd always expected.

Bollocks.

He stared at Sean's hands, still holding his. The strong fingers were tanned from distant sunshine and dark hair dusted the backs, thickening on his wiry forearms. Justin's breath caught as he was knocked sideways by want—for sex, yes, but also for something so much more. He ached for Sean to hold him, but he was too scared to ask for a hug in case it unlocked the emotions he was already struggling to contain.

"Are you hungry?" he asked instead, reluctantly detaching his hands from Sean's.

"Starving." Sean patted his belly. "I worked up quite an appetite last night." Justin raised an eyebrow, and Sean flushed and chuckled. "I meant from all the dancing. But yeah. That too."

"We can stay here and eat cornflakes and toast, or we could head out to a café for something more substantial."

Sean groaned appreciatively. "I'd kill for something involving bacon right now."

"Good idea." Justin only had a mild hangover, but there was nothing like a greasy fry-up after a night out. "Okay. You have first shower while I grab a coffee. Then we can head out in search of meat." Justin wiggled his eyebrows, unable to resist taking it further. "I quite fancy a sausage myself."

"You're so predictable." Sean rolled his eyes, but he laughed anyway.

"Meat jokes are always funny. Always have been, always will be. Now get your arse in the shower. If you're anything like me this morning, you're probably still a bit sticky." The words made his cheeks heat, but he refused to pretend last night hadn't happened. It might just be a memory, but Justin wasn't going to let Sean forget it.

"I'm more crusty than sticky." Sean wrinkled his nose.

"Nice." Justin stood. "Right, I need caffeine. Do you want another one?"

"No, I'm good, thanks."

Justin couldn't help the way his gaze skimmed down as Sean stood up, letting the blanket that had been draped over him drop. His focus caught on the bulge in Sean's boxers, and he had to turn away quickly as his dick thickened in response.

"Have a nice shower," he called back over his shoulder. "If you're going to have a wank, don't use all the hot water."

"I'll be quick," Sean said lightly.

God. Justin's cock was at full mast already from simply imagining it. He'd always fancied Sean, of course, but that was in a low-level, theoretical kind of a way. Nothing compared to the way his body reacted now he knew what he was missing. The sooner he could get in the shower and work off some sexual tension of his own, the better.

They went to the Unicorn Café again.

"I know it's a bit of a walk, but they do a really great breakfast," Justin said as they set out. "Way better than the greasy spoon on the corner of my road. Plus their coffee's better."

"Is it me, or is it colder today?" Sean pulled his hat down over his ears and turned up the collar of his coat.

"Yeah, it's freezing." Justin's breath made a plume in the chilly winter air. "I love it when it's like this, though. Feels like proper winter instead of the sad grey excuse we get for it in this country most of the time." He was glad he'd brought gloves, though, and he shoved his hands deep in his pockets too.

The café was warm, bright, and bustling with other people who'd had the same idea as them. The scent of bacon and coffee hit them as they approached, warm tendrils curling out into the frozen street and luring them in.

"Is there a table?" Sean asked looking around. "It's way too cold to sit outside."

Justin scanned the room. "I dunno. We could get a coffee and wait at the counter. Someone's bound to leave soon."

"We're nearly done." A black girl—probably in her teens—with a pierced nose and a beautiful smile put her hand on Justin's arm to get his attention. She was sitting with another girl who had peroxide blonde hair cut close to her scalp. Justin noticed they were holding hands. This was one of the reasons he loved this place. It was a safe space for people of all ages to be out and proud. "You go and order, and we'll save the table for you."

"Cheers," Justin said. "But don't rush. It looks like there's a queue, anyway."

They joined the line.

"I already know what I want," Justin said. "Full English for me."

Sean studied the menu written on a giant chalkboard over the counter. "Wow, they have a lot of choice. I quite fancy the breakfast burrito, or maybe the omelette… but full English is tempting too. I haven't had one since I got home."

When they reached the front of the queue, the guy taking the orders smiled at them both. Justin recognised him as Frank, the owner. The other bloke, who Justin thought was his partner, was also behind the counter, working the coffee machine. Dark and stocky, he was a little shorter than Frank.

"Hello again. What can I get for you boys?" Frank asked.

"Two full English breakfasts," Sean said. "And coffee for me, flat white. Justin? Coffee or tea?"

"White coffee for me too. And can I get an orange juice as well? Vitamin C's good for hangovers, right?"

"Like that, is it?" Frank chuckled. "Yeah, so they say. I hope it was worth it. Did you have a good night?"

Justin felt the smug grin of the sexually satisfied creep across his features. "Yeah. It was definitely worth it." He nudged Sean, who glanced sidelong at him, cheeks flushing as he smiled back.

Frank studied them both with a knowing expression, and Justin wondered what he was thinking. But Frank didn't comment. He turned to the man at the coffee machine and gave him the slip of paper with their drinks order. Justin noticed how Frank put a more-than-friendly hand on the dark guy's hip as he spoke to him, and they exchanged a smile that spoke of intimacy and affection.

"Thanks, baby," Frank said, patting the dark guy's arse as he turned back to Justin and Sean. "It's my husband's turn on coffee duty today."

Justin felt a pang of envy. He wanted what they had. He'd spent all his adult life so far looking for that kind of connection, and the only person he'd ever found it with was Sean rather than any of his lovers—his *other* lovers after last night, he supposed. Did Sean count as a lover if they'd only done it that one night?

Frank interrupted Justin's wonderings. "That'll be sixteen pounds fifty, please."

"I'll get this," Justin said as Sean reached in his pocket for his wallet.

"Let me give you my half."

"No. It's my treat." He knew Sean was skint. "You can buy me breakfast once you've got a job. Take me out to celebrate."

"I might not still be living in London by then."

Justin felt those words like a punch in the gut. He'd only just got Sean back in his life. He didn't want to lose him again so soon. "Well, in that case you'll have to come back and visit."

He took the change Frank offered, and Sean picked up the glass of orange juice.

"We'll bring your coffees over when they're ready," Frank said.

"Cheers." Justin pocketed his change.

The girls from before looked ready to leave. The one who'd spoken to them earlier caught their eye and gave a little wave.

"It's all yours," she said when they reached the table, standing and wrapping a colourful scarf around her neck.

"Thanks." Justin slid into the chair she'd vacated and Sean took the seat opposite. "Have a good day."

"You too."

Silence descended between them when the girls had gone. Sean sipped at his orange juice while Justin watched his hands again. It was impossible not to imagine them on his body now he knew how they felt.

"When are you going away for Christmas?" Sean asked once they had their coffees and plates of food.

"My flight's booked for the twenty-third." Justin paused between mouthfuls. "And I'm coming back on the twenty-seventh. What about you, have you made plans with your dad?"

Sean didn't meet his eyes. Looking down at his plate, he cut into a slice of bacon as he replied casually. "Yeah. I'm probably just going to go down there for a day or so, maybe stay two nights at the most."

"You sure you don't want to come with me to Scotland instead? My mum and dad would love to see you. You could catch up with your dad another time."

"No, it's fine. I ought to get it over with."

"Okay." Unease twisted in Justin's chest. He knew Sean had a difficult relationship with his dad.

He hadn't taken it well when Sean had finally told him about his sexuality, and Sean had hardly seen him since. But Christmas was the time for duty visits, and maybe they could build some bridges. At least Sean had Justin's place to escape to if it got too much.

CHAPTER TEN

Sean heard the sound of Justin's key in the door.

"Hi, honey, I'm home," Justin called as the front door slammed shut. "Wow. Something smells good." He came into the kitchen and grinned when he saw Sean at the cooker.

"Don't jinx it." Sean stirred the pan. "Your saucepan is shit and it keeps sticking."

A warm hand landed on his waist, and Justin's chin poked into his shoulder as he peered over. "What's for dinner?"

"Chilli."

Justin's hand lingered and Sean's skin tingled at the contact.

During the week since the party, they'd slipped back into their friendship as though nothing had happened, on the surface at least, but Sean hadn't been able to stop thinking about that night. He lay awake at night, burning with the desire to creep through the flat to Justin's bed and get his hands and mouth on him. So many times he'd thought about flirting, hinting, blatantly asking if they could do it again, but fear of damaging what they already had stopped him before the words formed on his lips.

Occasionally he caught Justin watching him, and he wondered whether Justin was thinking the same, but Sean was too afraid to ask. Even if the answer was yes, Sean wasn't sure he could have sex with Justin without strings attached. He wanted the strings; he needed them. The only way he could be with Justin was if he knew it was for keeps.

After dinner they slouched on the sofa together, watching some sci-fi movie on Netflix. Sean wasn't really following the plot, preoccupied by thoughts of Christmas. Justin was leaving the day after tomorrow, and Sean hadn't checked whether Justin would mind him crashing here while he was away.

"Is it okay if I stay here while you're in Scotland?"

"Of course." Justin's gaze was still on the screen. "You can spend as much time here as you need."

Sean bit his lip, then admitted, "I'm probably going to be here the whole time actually — if that's all right with you?"

"What?" Justin paused the film and turned, frowning. "Of course you can stay here, but I thought you had plans with your dad?"

Sean flushed. "Yeah. About that. I never got around to contacting him. He thinks I'm still abroad. I can't face seeing him yet."

Justin put his hand on Sean's thigh and squeezed. Sean swallowed against the lump in his throat, grateful for Justin's silent support. If anyone understood how difficult Sean found it to be around his father, it was Justin.

Sean's father's disapproval at his coming out had driven a wedge into their already fragile relationship. Sean almost wished he'd never told him, but he'd been tired of fielding questions about non-existent girlfriends, of pretending he was playing the field before he settled down. When Sean had told him the truth — that if he settled down with anyone, it was going to be another man — his dad's initial reaction had been one of denial and disbelief, swiftly replaced by anger and unhappiness when he realised Sean wasn't going to miraculously see the error of his ways. If he'd reached a place of acceptance, Sean hadn't been there to see it. He'd hardly contacted his dad while he was away beyond the occasional quick email to let him know he was still alive, and his dad's responses had been similarly brief.

"But you shouldn't be on your own for Christmas," Justin said. "Please come with me. My parents love you. They'll be thrilled."

Sean shook his head. "I can't afford the flight." Justin opened his mouth, but Sean cut in again. "And don't even think about offering to pay it for me. Anyway, it's probably too late to book now. You know what it's like at this time of year."

"But won't you be bored here on your own?"

Sean shrugged. "You've got video games I haven't played yet and there's Netflix. I think I'll cope. Plus I have plenty of job applications to keep me busy. I'll be fine."

"Okay," Justin said unhappily. He patted Sean's thigh. "If you're sure."

"I'm sure."

Sean didn't think he could handle spending Christmas with Justin and his parents anyway. It would only remind him of all the things he didn't have.

The following day Justin got home late.

"Bloody hell, I'm knackered. Thank God I'm finally on holiday. But my flight's tomorrow morning, and the last thing I feel like doing now is packing." He collapsed beside Sean on the sofa.

"Have you seen the weather forecast?" Sean asked. "Apparently there's snow coming our way, lots of it. It looks pretty bad."

"Fuck, really?" Justin sat up and pulled his phone out. "No, I didn't think to check. We hardly ever get snow before Christmas."

"Yeah, I saw it on the news at lunchtime. They're talking about flights being delayed — or even cancelled if the Met Office is right."

Justin opened his emails and found a message from his mum. He scanned her message, frowning. "They've got snow forecast up there too. Mum reckons they might be cut off for a few days if it comes. She says to check with them before I get on the plane, because they might not be able to get out to meet me at the airport even if I *can* still fly up. Bollocks."

"I'm sorry." Sean knew Justin had been looking forward to seeing his parents. Used to visiting them more frequently, he must be missing the contact since they'd moved north. "So, I might be stuck with you for Christmas, then?" Sean teased, trying to cheer him up.

"Looks that way." Justin seemed to perk up at that. "I guess I'll see what happens with the weather overnight before I make a final decision, but I think I'll hold off on packing till tomorrow morning. I'll get up early and see what's what."

Sean couldn't help a flicker of excitement at the prospect of Justin staying here after all. He felt a bit bad hoping that the promised snow would materialise, because he knew Justin would be disappointed not to see his family. Despite what he'd said to Justin, Sean hadn't been relishing the idea of spending Christmas alone.

The universe came down firmly on Sean's side. He woke to the sound of the kettle in the kitchen and Justin padding about in his socks.

When he looked at the clock on the TV, it was already half past nine. If Justin was flying out today, he should be on his way to the airport by now.

Sean sat up, yawned, and stretched till his back cracked. He climbed off the sofa bed, dragged a blanket around his shoulders, and went to open the curtains. "Wow!"

The city was covered with a thick white blanket of snow. It was still falling from the slate grey sky in feathery flakes that swirled hypnotically. There looked to be at least four inches already, judging by the tyres of the cars parked in the street below, and the clouds were heavy with more.

Justin came through from the kitchen and joined Sean at the window. "Sorry, I didn't know you were awake or I'd have made coffee for you too. You can share mine if you want."

Sean smiled at the giant mug in Justin's hands. "Looks like you've got enough for two anyway." He looked back out at the white rooftops. He couldn't remember when he'd last seen snow like this in England. It must've been several years, and never before Christmas. "So, you're not travelling today, then?"

"No." Justin sighed. "All flights are cancelled. I could go and wait and maybe fly out later today, or tomorrow. But Mum called me earlier, and apparently the roads are terrible up there. They did say they'd try and get to the airport if I could get a flight, but I told them not to risk it. I'm staying."

"That sucks," Sean said.

"Charming. I thought you'd be glad of the company." Justin nudged him.

"You know what I mean, dickhead." Sean nudged him back. "I know you were looking forward to seeing them."

"Oi, watch my coffee!" Justin put the mug down on the windowsill where the steam rose, clouding the glass like a warm breath. He met Sean's gaze and there was a softness to his features that made Sean's breath catch. "It's not so bad. I can visit them another time. I'm glad I get to stay here with you."

"Me too," Sean said gruffly.

"So." Justin's voice turned brisk. "We need a plan. The cupboards are bare, and I don't know what you were planning to eat for the next few days, but I'm buggered if I'll eat frozen pizza or Pot Noodle for Christmas dinner. If we're spending Christmas here, we're going to do it properly."

"That's going to involve me cooking, right?" Sean raised an eyebrow.

Justin's skills in the kitchen were limited to making wicked coffee and heating things up.

"I think it will go better if you're in charge. But I'm really good at peeling things." Justin's grin was hopeful, and happiness rose in Sean as he started to think about how much fun it would be spending Christmas with him.

"We'll need decorations too." Sean sat down on the edge of the sofa bed and picked up a pad of paper and a pen from the coffee table.

"What are you doing?"

"Making a list."

"Of course you are." Justin moved to sit beside him, coffee mug in his hands. The bed creaked under the added weight. He leaned in to see, and Sean could smell the scent of his hair. He wanted to turn and bury his nose in it, put an arm around Justin, and pull him close.

Instead he started writing: *Turkey? Or chicken? Potatoes, parsnips, stuffing —*

"We have to have turkey, or it won't feel like Christmas," Justin said.

"Turkey crown, then," Sean suggested. "Unless you want to be eating turkey for the next month." He put the pen and pad down and took the mug out of Justin's hands for a sip.

Justin picked up the list and took over the job of writing. "Okay. What else do we need?"

By the time they'd finished, the mug was empty, the shopping list was ridiculously long, and Sean was feeling more excited about Christmas than he had done in years. Maybe since his mum died.

They decided to get all the shopping done that day. There was a supermarket close by where they could get everything they needed.

"What about presents?" Justin said.

They didn't normally exchange gifts. By unspoken agreement over the years, the most they'd ever done was give each other a card — usually handmade, featuring whichever cartoon or video game characters they were into at the time.

Sean frowned, considering. "It's Christmas. We need something to open, but can we keep it cheap? I don't want you to spend much on me." By the time they'd split the grocery bill, he wouldn't have much left to play with.

"Okay, how about a ten-quid limit?" Justin suggested, eyes bright with enthusiasm.

"Done."

Sean was relieved that the grocery shopping didn't come to as much as he'd expected, thanks to all the Christmas special offers. The decorations were reduced to clear, so they ended up with a metric fuckton of tinsel, some baubles, several sets of fairy lights, and a small fake Christmas tree to set up in the corner of Justin's lounge.

When Sean got his wallet out at the till to give Justin his contribution to the cost, Justin wouldn't let Sean pay for half the decorations. "They're for my flat. Don't be daft."

"But they were my idea."

"I don't care." Justin had a stubborn set to his jaw, so Sean gave up arguing.

He did a quick mental calculation as he pulled some cash out of his wallet.

"Well, this is for my half of the food, then."

"It's okay. Pay me when you get a job," Justin said, looking doubtful. "There's no rush."

"It's fine. Take it." Sean shoved the folded notes into the front pocket of Justin's jeans, and the backs of his fingers bumped against Justin's hipbone. Their gazes locked and Justin's eyes widened, his pupils dark despite the bright supermarket lighting. Sean pulled away and started packing their shopping into carrier bags.

Back at Justin's flat they unpacked the groceries and then had a quick bite to eat before heading out to buy gifts for each other in the afternoon.

"Let's split up. Text each other when we're done, and we can meet for coffee?" Justin suggested.

"Okay."

Sean wandered the busy shops, hoping inspiration would strike. He had no ideas, but he reckoned he'd find something that would catch his interest if he browsed. There were a thousand different gift ideas on display. He considered books, CDs, mugs, T-shirts with funny slogans, but nothing grabbed him.

Then, walking past the children's toy section in a department store, he caught sight of the perfect gift — a display of soft toys with every type of animal you could imagine. The ones that caught Sean's eye were strung along the top of the display. Orangutans, lemurs, and several different types of monkey hung from a fake vine in a variety of positions. Sean went straight for the ones he recognised as gibbons. There was a black one and a golden one, so he chose the golden one because it reminded him of Justin. The price tag said £9.99. It was obviously meant to be.

"Perfect," he muttered with a grin on his face.

He paid for it, along with a sheet of wrapping paper, and made sure it was well tucked away in the bottom of the carrier bag so that Justin wouldn't be able to see what it was. Then he texted Justin to let him know he was done.

Justin replied with *Ugh, still looking. Too many things. Meet u back home later instead? All the cafes will be rammed anyway.*

Sure, Sean replied. He'd had enough of shops for one day. This way he could wrap his gift up before Justin got back.

Snow was still falling as he walked back to the Tube. A gritter lorry roared past, spitting out dirty salt onto the slush where the snow had been churned up by the traffic. More snow was forecast for tonight, and it was supposed to freeze hard too.

Sean was glad they didn't have to go anywhere for a few days. He'd been blessed with a white Christmas in the company of the person he loved best in the world. It could only be more perfect if Justin loved him back the same way.

Sean gave a wistful sigh. Maybe miracles could happen.

Back at the flat, Sean wrapped his present before Justin came home, and tucked it away in the bottom of his rucksack ready for Christmas.

Justin finally showed up a couple of hours later. He went straight to his room before Sean could catch a glimpse of the bags he was carrying, and then came back and collapsed on the sofa with a sigh.

"Bloody hell, I'm knackered."

Sean grinned. "All shopped out?"

"Yeah. I'm starving too."

"Want me to feed you?" Sean asked.

"Yes please."

Sean cooked pasta for dinner. After they'd eaten, they got sucked into a *Call of Duty* marathon that took up the rest of the evening and went on past midnight. When Sean finally got into bed, he fell asleep almost immediately.

CHAPTER ELEVEN

The next morning Justin bounced onto the sofa bed beside Sean. "Wake up!" He prodded Sean's sleeping form.

Sean raised his head and rubbed his bleary eyes, his dark curls a hot mess and his cheeks flushed with sleep. "Where's the fire?" he mumbled.

"We've got lots to do today," Justin said. "Fuck, it's cold. Move over."

Sean shifted obligingly, and Justin got under the covers beside him and snuggled close, grateful for the heat of Sean's body as he put an arm around Justin. Dressed only in boxers and a T-shirt, Justin was freezing. The heating took a while to get going in the morning when it was really cold outside.

"What's the plan?" Sean asked.

"We need to decorate the flat."

"That won't take long."

"But first I want to go and play in the snow. There's even more today, and we didn't get to have any fun with it yesterday. We should go to the park and make a snowman, or maybe a snow penis. Oooh, we should totally do that! We could put it on Instagram and see if it goes viral."

"You're such a kid." Sean's voice was teasing.

Justin poked him in the ribs, meeting firm flesh where Sean's T-shirt was rucked up. "Adulting is overrated."

"Shit, your hands are cold." Sean tried to push him away, but Justin rolled on top of him and shoved his icy hands under Sean's T-shirt. His skin was

103

warm and the hair on his belly felt good against Justin's palms.

Sean fought him off, flipping Justin over and pinning his wrists over his head. His knee ended up between Justin's legs, his thigh pressing down against Justin's cock. Surrounded by Sean's sweet, musky scent, with the weight of Sean's body pinning him to the bed, Justin froze. The heat of arousal combined with embarrassment ripped through him as he felt himself harden against Sean's hip.

"Um." Justin squirmed, not sure if he was trying to escape or rub up against that hard, muscled thigh like a randy dog. Maybe a bit of both.

"Oh."

Sean stared down at him, tangled curls falling into his eyes, his expression suddenly intense as Justin stared back, unable to look away, paralysed by that gaze like a butterfly on a pin.

Sean swallowed, and Justin wanted to lick his throat, to feel the movement under his tongue. He hesitated, trapped by uncertainty. Before he could think of words or actions that might turn this moment into something more, Sean released his wrists.

"Sorry." He rolled off Justin and lay on his back beside him.

"Morning wood. It happens." Justin gestured vaguely at his crotch, cheeks still flaming.

"Yeah. Yeah, of course." Sean scrubbed his hands over his face.

Justin felt the pulse between his legs, his dick throbbing in time to the beat of his heart. He broke the silence before it could get any more awkward. "You want coffee?"

"Please."

Justin got out of the bed and went to the kitchen without looking back. He needed to get a grip. Sean was his friend, the friend he'd had one amazing night with, but it seemed that was all it was ever going to be. Sean might be moving away soon. Even if he stayed in London, he hadn't given any real indication that he wanted more than friendship from Justin, and Justin wasn't brave enough to ask.

They made it to the park a few streets away by about half nine in the morning, early enough that the snow was still relatively unspoilt. A few kids were out with their parents, making snowmen and having snowball fights, but there was still plenty of pristine white snow that hadn't been marked by footprints yet. It glittered as the pale morning sunshine poured from the blue winter sky.

Justin marched over to a quiet corner of the park, packed a lump of snow in his hands until it was about the size of a cannonball, then put it down and started to roll it.

"Snowman?" Sean asked.

"Nope. Snow dick, of course."

"Seriously?" Sean looked around. "There are children present."

"They won't be able to tell what it is from a distance. Don't be such a spoilsport." Justin's first snowball was now about the size of a basketball. "That'll do," he said. "Now we just need a few more like that. We'll stick them together in a tower, and we can sculpt it to make it smooth."

"You're an embarrassment," Sean grumbled, but he joined in, shaping some snow in his gloves and then stooping to roll it into a larger ball.

Justin grinned, amused by Sean's reluctance. Justin had always been the one to lead him astray. Good to see some things never changed.

Once they'd stacked several snowballs together and smoothed them into a column, they had some artistic differences. They argued for a while about whether the snow dick should be cut or uncut.

"Cut's easier," Sean said. "Less fiddly and it will look more obviously like a dick if we can shape the head."

Apparently Sean's reluctance about Project Snow Peen had evaporated once his creative instincts had kicked in. Justin chuckled. "This isn't America, Sean. Anyway, it's clearly erect, so the foreskin can be pulled back. You get shaping. I'm going to start making the bollocks."

By the time they'd finished, even Justin had to admit it was pretty pornographic in its anatomical detail. Thankfully nobody had come close enough to see what they were doing.

"It's a thing of beauty," Sean said, standing back, his arms folded as they studied it.

"It really is." Justin got out his phone. He took photos from every conceivable angle. "I'll put the best one on Instagram later. Hashtag: snowdickpic. Maybe I can get it trending."

"Oh God, there are kids coming," Sean said in alarm. "Can we leave now, please? Either that or I'm going to put a face on it and add some sticks for arms."

"No!" Justin said in mock horror. "You can't ruin it. It's art. Leave it for posterity or until it melts or gets stomped on. But yeah, let's go. My gloves are soaked through and my toes are frozen. I think my boots leaked."

When they got home, Sean folded his bed back into sofa form while Justin turned the heating up and made hot chocolate for them. Then they snuggled on the sofa under blankets while they thawed out.

"My feet are still like ice blocks," Justin complained. "My circulation is shit." He wiggled his toes against Sean's thigh where he sat at the opposite end. He could still hardly feel them. "I need a hot water bottle or something."

"Here." Sean set his mug down and pulled Justin's feet into his lap. He stripped the sock off one foot and rubbed it between his hands, which were warm from holding his drink. "Bloody hell, they are freezing."

Sean wrapped his hands around Justin's foot and held it tight, letting the warmth seep into Justin's icy skin. Then he rubbed it again until Justin felt the tingle of blood coming back to the surface with the familiar stinging feeling associated with being too cold for too long. Once that foot thawed out, Sean swapped and did the other one. But his hands were cold from the first foot now, so it took longer for the friction of his hands to work. The rubbing turned into a foot massage. Justin lay back and closed his eyes, mind drifting as he lost himself in the sensation of Sean's thumbs working the arch of his foot. He only came back to himself when Sean patted his leg.

"You okay now?"

"Yeah, thanks." Justin opened his eyes, blinking at the brightness. He yawned and stretched. "I'm ready for a nap."

"Oh no. No way. Not after you woke me up at what-the-fuck o'clock to go and make snow penises.

I'm wide awake now, so you're not going back to bed. We've got decorating to do, remember?"

"Oh, yes." Justin perked up, excited at the thought of making his flat look festive. "Where are my socks?"

"Here." Sean threw them at his head and Justin caught them, laughing.

"So helpful."

An hour and a half later they were done.

Justin turned the main lights off, plunging the flat into dusky gloom. Although it was only lunchtime, it had clouded over again outside, and the sky was the sort of dirty grey that usually heralded more snow.

"Ready?" Sean asked, finger paused over the switch that would turn the Christmas lights on—one set on the tree, another other draped over the mantelpiece, and a third that they'd wrapped around the standard lamp in the corner of the room.

"I feel like we should have invited a minor celebrity over to switch them on for us," Justin said.

Sean chuckled. "Plenty of them around in London. I'm sure we could have got one of them to take a break from their hectic panto schedule. But it's too late now, so you're gonna have to make do with me. Okay. Three, two, one…." He hit the lights.

Justin breathed out a happy sigh, a smile spreading across his face. He'd always adored the strings of fairy lights that his family put up every Christmas. Of all the decorations, they were the ones he loved the most. Their soft light transformed the mundane into something magical. The tinsel on the tree caught the light, and the silver and gold baubles gleamed, tiny mirrors reflecting the different colours like a shattered rainbow.

"It's beautiful." Happiness rose in his chest, light and bubbly as he stepped forward to admire the tree.

Sean came and stood beside him. "Yeah. It really is."

On an impulse, Justin put an arm around Sean's waist and brushed a quick, chaste kiss against his cheek. "I'm really glad you're here. It would suck to be stuck here alone for Christmas."

Sean put his arm around Justin's shoulders and squeezed. "I'm glad I'm here too."

They stared at the tree in silence for a little while longer, but then Justin's stomach rumbled and reminded him that it was past one o'clock. "Let's get some lunch, then we can chill. I fancy some of that Mario and Sonic game this afternoon—you know, the one at the Olympics with all the skiing and snowboarding."

They gathered up the empty bags and boxes that had held the decorations.

"We forgot to put these ones up." Sean held up another box of fairy lights.

"Oh, I kept those to go over my bed." Justin took them. "I've always wanted some. I might leave them up all year round."

Sean smirked.

"What?" Justin demanded. "Fairy lights are awesome."

"But over your bed? What are you, a thirteen-year-old girl?"

"Fuck off." Justin flipped him the finger. "I'm secure enough in my masculinity that I can indulge my love of pretty things. I'm sad for you that you have to prove yourself by living a life devoid of beauty."

"Yeah, yeah. Whatever. Now, what's for lunch?"

They spent the afternoon playing in virtual snow on the Wii rather than in the real stuff. When they were tired of snowboarding, skiing, and figure skating, they put some mince pies in the oven to warm up.

"I think it's beer o'clock," Sean suggested.

"Beer doesn't go with mince pies. I fancy some red wine."

"Oh yeah. That sounds good."

Justin opened a bottle and was pouring them both glasses when the oven timer went off. They carried everything to the coffee table and took up residence on the sofa again.

Justin turned on the TV and found that *Love Actually* had just started.

Sean groaned. "You're going to make me watch this aren't you?"

"Yep." Justin loved romcoms. Always had, always would. There was something about watching other people get happy endings that gave him hope. Maybe one day he'd finally find a nice guy whom he'd love more than Sean and who could cure him of his terminal crush.

Once they'd demolished the mince pies, Justin pulled the blanket off the back of the sofa and spread it over them both, moving closer to Sean.

"You cold again?" Sean lifted his arm obligingly, letting Justin slide underneath it to snuggle.

"A bit," Justin lied. He was perfect. But he had to take his chances to get close to Sean wherever he could find them.

They spent the rest of the evening on the sofa, indulging in a Christmas movie marathon. They finished the first bottle of wine and opened a second, but they slowed down, only getting halfway through that bottle by the time *The Holiday* had finished.

Justin yawned, but stayed put as the finished credits rolled. Warm and comfortable with his head in Sean's lap and Sean's fingers idly stroking his hair, he didn't want to move. He could lie like this forever. He glanced up at Sean's face, the strong jaw covered with stubble, the way his dark eyes glittered in the fairy lights. Justin's stomach did a pathetic little flop of longing, hopeless, like a stranded fish.

Sean looked down at him and Justin held his gaze, wishing, but not daring to hope.

Sean cleared his throat, and his voice was soft and husky when he spoke. "It feels like we're pretending to be boyfriends again."

Justin's heart surged, pounding in double time as he studied Sean's face, searching for something, anything to give him the courage to ask for what he wanted. The tenderness he saw there made the words come.

"We could try it again," he managed, his voice small, strangled by emotion too strong to contain. "I liked being boyfriends."

Sean's chest lifted, his breath coming faster. "Me too," he whispered.

Justin was almost afraid to move, terrified of getting it wrong and breaking the spell between them. But he forced himself to be brave. He lifted his hand and touched Sean's cheek, caressing the scruff on his jaw as he asked, "If you were my boyfriend. What would you do next?"

Sean licked his lips. "I'd kiss you."

Justin felt as though the world stopped and waited. Caught in the moment, they stared at each other, utterly still. And then suddenly they both moved at once, Sean lowering his head as Justin pushed up on his elbows. Their mouths met in a graceless smash of lips and clack of teeth, and their noses bumped painfully.

They pulled apart, both laughing as Sean rubbed his nose.

Fuck it. Justin wasn't letting this slip away from him. He sat up and got into Sean's lap, straddling him and grinning down at Sean's surprised face. "Call that a kiss?"

This time Justin took control, claiming Sean's mouth and kissing him deep and dirty. Sean brought his arms up and held Justin close, his hands sliding under Justin's T-shirt and over his skin, making Justin moan and grind down on the hard bulge in Sean's sweatpants.

Sean dragged his lips away from Justin's, scratching his thick stubble over Justin's softer two-day growth. "God, Justin," he muttered as he sucked on Justin's neck. He was probably pulling a mark to the surface, but Justin couldn't bring himself to care.

"What else?" Justin asked breathlessly.

"Huh?" Sean sucked again, harder.

"What else would you do? If we were a couple? Oh—"

Sean worked a hand down the front of Justin's pyjama bottoms and circled his cock with a firm grip, tugging and stroking. He drew back, pupils blown with desire, lips wet from their kisses. "I'd ask you to take me to bed and fuck me." He carried on stroking Justin as he spoke.

Justin stared at him. "You'd want me to top?" His cock pulsed in Sean's hand, pushing out a bead of precome, apparently on board with this plan. "Wow. I always figured you'd be a top."

"I don't bottom that often, because I only like it with someone I really trust." Sean flushed. "But my prostate is really sensitive. So I'm kind of a cock slut when I get the chance."

"Fuck." Justin reached down and gripped Sean's wrist. "You can't say stuff like that to me while you're jerking me off. Not if you want me to actually get my dick in your arse." He searched Sean's face for a sign that this was going to happen, that it wasn't just dirty talk while they fooled around on the sofa. He couldn't tell. "Do you want to go and, um, do that?"

"If you do?"

"Fuck, *yes*."

Sean chuckled at his enthusiasm. "Have you got lube and condoms?"

"In the bedroom." Justin scrambled off Sean's lap and held out a hand to pull him up.

In Justin's room, Sean stripped to his boxers while Justin got out the supplies. Then Sean gestured to the bathroom door. "I'm just gonna go clean up a bit."

"Need any help?" Justin grinned.

Sean rolled his eyes. "Uh. No. Not my kink. Back in a few."

Justin turned on the string of fairy lights he'd draped over the headboard and turned off the normal lamp. Then he got naked and slipped under the covers. His cock brushed against the sheets as he settled on his back, still hard despite the break in the proceedings. He took himself in hand and stroked slowly, listening to the sound of the shower running. The bed warmed around him as he moved his hand over his cock, not close to coming but ready to get straight back to business.

Sean came back a few minutes later. His hair was dry, but he had a towel around his waist. Justin lifted up the covers for him. When Sean dropped the towel, Justin let his gaze lock on to Sean's cock. It was soft, but it thickened and rose as Justin stared.

"Fuck, you're gorgeous." Justin moved over to make space. He ran his hand down Sean's flank, reaching around to squeeze his arse. His fingers slipped into the damp crack and Sean threw his leg over Justin's hip, opening up for him. "Let me get the lube."

He opened Sean up like that. Not the easiest position for access, but it meant he could kiss him while he did it, and he didn't think he'd ever get tired of kissing Sean. Sean's mouth opened for Justin's tongue as his hole softened under Justin's fingers, little needy moans and gasps escaping as Justin worked his fingers into him, stretching his rim and getting him ready.

When Justin sensed that Sean was getting impatient, he eased his fingers out and patted Sean on the hip. "You ready? Pass me a condom."

Sean rolled it on for him, and Justin bit his lip at the stroke of his hand.

"Okay, how do you want to do this?" Justin asked.

Sean rolled onto his stomach, kicking the covers down. He tucked a pillow under his hips, spread his thighs and tilted his arse up. "Like this."

Justin moved to kneel between Sean's legs, admiring the view for a moment. He felt as though all his Christmases had come at once.

Sean gripped his buttocks, holding himself open like a gift. "Justin." The thread of need in his voice made Justin's balls draw up.

"Fuck, okay." Justin lined up and rubbed the tip of his cock over Sean's hole. For a moment Sean's body resisted. "Come on, baby. Let me in." Justin pushed a little harder, then gasped as Sean's muscles relaxed and he eased into the tight, grasping heat.

Sean made a high keening sound and Justin froze, afraid he was uncomfortable. But Sean pushed back, forcing Justin in deep.

They both cursed.

"Yeah. God, that's perfect. Do it. Fuck me." Sean's head was turned to one side and Justin could see the flush on his cheeks, the slack of his mouth where he gasped the words against the sheet.

Justin braced his arms on either side of Sean's body and started to fuck, hard and fast, because that was what Sean seemed to want.

Sean moaned with every thrust, the sounds knocked out of him as Justin slammed in. He hoped the angle was good for Sean. "This okay?" he managed.

"It's fucking brilliant."

But it was going to be over all too soon. Sean was hot and tight and the sight of him spread out, begging for Justin to fuck him was too much. The electric tingle of impending release built, pooling in Justin's balls and trickling up his spine.

"I need a timeout. Otherwise I'm going to come," he warned.

"No! Don't stop." Sean rocked his hips, grinding back on each thrust. "Don't you fucking dare... even *think* about stopping...." His words trailed off in a hoarse cry of pure pleasure and his walls pulsed around Justin as he came, hips jerking into the pillow. Justin pressed in deep and let Sean ride it out until the tension left his body and he relaxed.

Justin drew out and then pushed back in, hoping he could finish now, but Sean hissed. "I'm really sensitive after coming. You'll need to go carefully."

"It's okay." Justin was so close. It wasn't going to take much, but waiting wasn't an option and he didn't trust himself not to hurt Sean if he carried on. He pulled out carefully and sat back on his heels. He stroked himself over the condom a few times before pausing to pull it off.

Sean looked over his shoulder. "Need some help? Want my mouth?"

"Nah." Justin started stroking again. "You can just lie there and look pretty." He parted Sean's cheeks with his free hand so he could see his hole, all pink and shiny with lube. He made a grunt of appreciation, stroking his cock harder, faster. "Oh fuck, yeah."

He came with a strangled groan, hips snapping forward as he fucked into his fist, painting Sean's gorgeous arse with thick white streaks. One landed right next to his crack, and Justin caught it with his thumb, smearing it over Sean's hole.

"You kinky bastard," Sean said, grinning from ear to ear.

"Apparently." Justin had never had a thing for come play before, yet something about Sean made him want to push his spunk inside him and leave it there.

"Clean me up, you fucker. I want to roll over so I can kiss you again."

Justin reached for the tissues beside the bed and wiped his mess off Sean.

"Cheers." Sean rolled over, pulling the pillow out from under his hips. "I don't think tissues will be much help for this wet patch, though." He flipped the pillow over and rested his head on the dry side, reaching up for Justin's hand so he could pull him down. "C'mere."

Sean wrapped his arms around Justin, and they kissed, slowly and lazily. Sean stroked his hands over Justin's back, and Justin burrowed closer, losing himself in the warm strength of Sean's body and the sweetness of their kisses.

Outside in the streets, church bells pealed, the tumbling notes heralding the turn of midnight and the arrival of Christmas ringing out in celebration across the city.

Justin drew back so he could see Sean's face. Sean's dark eyes were soft and his lips swollen from kissing. He made Justin's heart twist.

"Merry Christmas," Justin whispered.

Sean smiled. "It's shaping up to be a great one. Merry Christmas."

CHAPTER TWELVE

Sean slipped into consciousness to the sensation of fingers combing through his hair. A warm body was pressed up behind him and humid breath washed over the bare skin of his shoulder.

He smiled as he remembered the night before and then braced himself, waiting for the doubts and uncertainty to sweep in, tarnishing the memory of what they'd done.

None came.

It felt so right, deep down in his bones and in his blood. He couldn't regret any of it, but they needed to talk.

He stretched, making a satisfied humming noise as he turned into Justin's arms, smiling sleepily.

"Morning," he said.

"Morning." Justin smiled back. He leaned in for a kiss, just a soft brush of lips. But as their bodies pressed together, Sean felt Justin's erection against his hip. He reached down and stroked it, raising an eyebrow. "Been awake long?"

Justin ran a hand over Sean's chest, thumbing his nipple until it hardened. "Not very." He lowered his voice into a husky confession. "I was thinking about last night."

"I figured." Sean squeezed Justin's cock, loving the heat of it in his hand. His mouth watered, spurring him into action. Talking could wait. He shuffled down beneath the covers, into the dark warm cave that smelled of both of them. His own cock hardened as he buried his nose in Justin's pubes. "You stink of sex." He breathed in deeply.

"You say that like it's a bad thing." Justin's voice was muffled by the duvet.

Sean tugged the covers down to his shoulders so he could see better. He glanced up at Justin and grinned. "It's not. Definitely not."

He turned his attention back to Justin's cock, guiding it into his mouth and sucking, lightly at first, until Justin started making impatient noises and tightened his fingers in Sean's hair.

Sean rolled him onto his back and took charge. He gave Justin what he wanted, sucking him deep and strong until Justin was cursing, breath coming in gasps. "Fuck, Sean. Yes. *Fuck*."

Justin thrust up into Sean's willing throat, pulsing and filling Sean's mouth with his come. When he was done, Sean released him, swallowing. He wrinkled his nose at the salty bitterness.

Justin chuckled. "You don't have to swallow if you don't like it. I don't care."

"Saves on mess."

"Says the guy who jizzed all over my pillow last night while he humped it like a dog."

Sean's cheeks heated, and mingled arousal and self-consciousness flooded through him as he remembered being arse up for Justin, begging for it.

Justin must have seen his slight discomfort because he reached up and pulled Sean down, his hand curled tight around Sean's nape so he couldn't look away. "Hey, you were amazing. Hottest fucking thing ever." He got his other hand on Sean's cock and stroked, his thumb slipping through the moisture at the tip. "You're sticky."

"Uh-huh."

"Well, roll over and let me blow you." Justin pushed at Sean's shoulder.

Sean obliged. "If you insist."

"It's traditional to exchange gifts at Christmas." Justin knelt between Sean's thighs and lowered his mouth to lick away the shiny bead of precome.

Sean's brain left the building. His head thudded back on the pillows, and he gave himself up to the pure, mind-blowing pleasure of Justin's mouth.

Afterwards they lay side by side. Justin's eyes were closed, but Sean stared at the ceiling, his mind whirling with questions. There were so many things he wanted to ask, but they all boiled down to one thing.

"What are we doing?" he finally asked.

Justin shifted beside him, propping himself up on one elbow. He looked down at Sean and shrugged one shoulder as he gave Sean a wry smile. "I dunno. It's fun though."

Sean couldn't deny that, even if he feared it was the sort of fun that could end in heartache. "I know, but...."

Justin cut in. "Let's enjoy it for now. It doesn't have to mean anything."

But it does, Sean wanted to say. *It means everything*.

Instead he followed Justin's lead. "What happens at Christmas stays at Christmas?" His gut twisted as he said the words.

Justin flopped back down onto the mattress again. Sean couldn't see his expression. "Something like that." He patted Sean's belly. "We'll work it out."

They exchanged non-blowjob-related gifts after breakfast. Justin wanted to open the presents they'd bought for each other straight away, but Sean insisted on coffee first, and then they both realised they were hungry.

Once they'd eaten, they went and sat in the living room with their second cups of coffee. Justin opened the curtains to a glorious blue sky. Sun poured in, making the tinsel on the tree reflect tiny points of light onto the ceiling.

Distracted by the sofa snogging that had led to sex, they'd forgotten to put their gifts under the tree last night, so they got them out now.

"Put them by the tree so I can take a photo. I want to send it to Mum to show her I decorated," Justin said. "Then she'll stop feeling bad about me being stuck here."

Sean got his hastily wrapped present out and put it under the tree alongside the one Justin had placed there. Both parcels were indeterminate shapes. Sean had wrapped his in boring gold paper, whereas Justin had gone for paper decorated with cartoon Santas and reindeer. Justin's was a little bigger, and when Sean prodded it, it rustled.

"Get your hand out of the way," Justin said, phone poised. Then came the click of the camera. "There."

"Can I open it now?" Sean was excited. He'd forgotten the thrill of unknown presents hiding inside wrapping paper. It had been a few years since he'd had anything other than a cheque from his dad.

"Yeah, go on, then. Don't get too excited, though. It's just a bit of fun."

Sitting cross-legged on the floor by the tree, Sean tore into the paper like an impatient kid. Justin had used a lot of tape, and bits of shredded paper fell to the floor as Sean ripped into it. Inside there was another layer—tissue paper this time, which explained the rustling.

"What is this, pass the parcel?" Sean looked up at Justin, who was watching him, grinning.

"Ooh, good idea. I should have put forfeits between the layers: take off an item of clothing, do a naked dance, blow me...."

"I've already done that today." Sean went back to unwrapping.

The tape came off the tissue paper easily, but loads of it was wrapped around the thing inside. When Sean finally got to it, he stared at the contents with a smile of disbelief spreading over his face. What were the chances?

"It's a—" Justin began.

"A gibbon. I know." Sean was laughing now, lifting out the black-haired gibbon by its ridiculously long arms and holding it as though it was hanging from a tree branch. "It's awesome. It's just...."

"What?" Justin was smiling at his reaction, but his brow was wrinkled with confusion. "It reminded me of you."

Sean chuckled again. "No spoilers. Open yours."

Justin reached for his present, and when he settled back opposite Sean, he was close enough that their knees bumped.

"Oh my God!" Justin pulled the golden-furred gibbon out of the paper and held it up, mimicking Sean's previous pose. "That's so fucking *weird*."

"I know. Great minds, huh?"

"We clearly know each other far too well." They grinned at each other, happiness swelling and filling the space between them. "Thank you." Justin crawled forward on his hands and knees and kissed Sean softly on the mouth. It was the first time they'd kissed like this—like boyfriends—outside of sex or Justin's bed. Sean's breath caught as the weight of hope and uncertainty slammed into his chest.

They needed to talk. He needed to know what this was, what Justin thought about it, but he didn't want to spoil Christmas by dragging this beautiful shining thing between them out into the open. He was afraid that, like fairy lights on a tree in the daytime, it would be washed out, weakened if they looked at it too closely.

Sean wasn't ready to let go of the illusion yet.

"Where are we going to put these guys, then?" He held up his gibbon.

"On the tree? Or we could hang them from the curtain rail."

They ended up hanging them by their Velcro feet and linking their arms so they were holding each other too.

Justin snapped a photo and put it on Instagram. "Here we go. Hashtag: xmasmonkeybusiness." He showed the photo to Sean.

"Does anyone else even use that hashtag?"

"Not yet. I like to be ahead of the curve."

They Skyped Justin's parents later in the morning. Justin insisted that Sean come and said hello, dragging him down on the sofa beside him as the call connected. He slung his arm around Sean's shoulders as though to stop him escaping.

"Hi!" Justin waved at the screen where his parents smiled back.

Sean grinned at their familiar faces. It had been way too long since he'd seen them. "Liz, Matthew… long time, no see."

After hellos and Christmas greetings, they chatted for a while. Justin's parents were on their own for Christmas because Justin's sister, Suzie, hadn't been able to make the journey either.

"We'll be eating turkey leftovers for the next month," Liz said. "Good thing we've got a big freezer."

"Is Suzie on her own?" Justin asked.

"No, she got invited to spend Christmas with a colleague. She threatened to try and drive up, but I talked her out of it," Liz said. "We can get together another time. I didn't want her to risk getting stranded. The snow's been really bad around the Lake District."

"Probably for the best, then."

"Yes. But I'm glad none of us are spending Christmas alone. Are you boys having fun?"

Justin tightened his arm around Sean's shoulder. "Yeah, we're doing fine. I couldn't ask for better company."

"I thought you'd be with your dad, Sean? Were the trains not running?"

"Um, I'm not sure…. I just figured it would be easier to visit him when the snow's gone." Sean shifted uncomfortably. He resented the guilt he felt for not contacting his dad. It wasn't like his dad had been in touch with him either.

"So, Mum, I meant to ask you. How do we cook a turkey crown? Is it the same calculation as you use for a whole turkey?" Justin deftly swooped to his rescue, and Sean was grateful. He didn't want to think about his dad today.

As he listened to Liz rattling on about meat thermometers and skewering the meat to check the juices, he found himself wondering what his dad would think if he knew about him and Justin. His dad had never liked Justin, and he'd liked him even less after he came out and started wearing T-shirts with unicorns on them and rainbow laces in his Converse.

Luckily Sean was old enough and thick-skinned enough now that he didn't give a flying fuck what his dad thought. If this fling with Justin turned into more, his dad was going to have to put up with it or get out of his life for good.

Christmas Day was perfect.

It wasn't perfect in that nothing went wrong — they burned the potatoes, because they underestimated the time for the turkey crown, and the gravy had lumps in it. Then the food was ready later than planned, so by the time they finally dished up Christmas dinner they'd eaten too many mince pies and were pissed on the sherry that Justin had insisted on buying.

Despite all that, Sean had never enjoyed a meal more. Sitting at the desk they'd set up as a dining table, he watched Justin opposite him. The flickering golden light from the candle softened Justin's angular features and made his hair gleam. Unguarded, Sean stared at him, allowing himself to be happy in the moment, refusing to think about what-ifs and what-nexts.

Justin glanced up and caught Sean's gaze, and he smiled. "You okay?"

"Yeah. Better than okay. Thanks for today, for everything. For letting me stay."

"No need for thanks. You know you're welcome, right?"

"You're the best." More words rose, fighting to the surface, and Sean's voice was rough as he added, "Love you." He couldn't look Justin in the eye as he said it. He knew Justin would hear the words but not the depth of the feelings behind them.

"Love you too." Justin kicked him lightly under the table and left his foot there, hooked around Sean's ankle while they finished eating.

After dinner they left the washing-up and collapsed onto the sofa.

"Ugh. I need to get out of these jeans, but I'm too full to move again," Justin complained.

"Undo the button?"

"Already done, halfway through the Christmas pudding. It's not enough."

"Take them off, then," Sean said.

"This is the best thing about spending Christmas with you. It's clothing optional." Justin wriggled out of his jeans and kicked them onto the floor. "Oh God, that's better. I recommend it."

So Sean took his trousers off too, and they cuddled under the sofa blanket, spooned together, with Sean behind. Justin grabbed his arm and pulled it around him, holding Sean's hand against his chest.

"Can we watch *The Sound of Music*?" Justin asked.

"Really?" Sean sighed.

"Please? It reminds me of being a kid. It doesn't feel like Christmas without it. Then after we can watch *The Wizard of Oz*. Tempting though the partial nudity going on under this blanket is, I'm too full to do anything more exciting than watch TV."

"Is this part of the whole pretend-boyfriend thing?" Sean joked as Justin scrolled through his recordings and lined up the first film. "Although I feel more like an old married couple now. Maybe this is my future." He meant it in general terms rather than with Justin specifically, but then his stomach lurched when he realised how it sounded.

"Hey, you'd be lucky to have a future this awesome," Justin said lightly.

Sean breathed a sigh of relief. "Yeah. I guess it wouldn't be so bad. But I'd rather we were watching *The Avengers*." He snuggled closer and breathed in the scent of Justin's hair. It was addictive. He wasn't a fan of either of Justin's film choices, but he was okay with the idea of a nap with Justin in his arms. Full of food and sleepy from drinking all afternoon, he was asleep before Maria even reached the Von Trapp house.

Sean woke hours later with a crick in his neck. The TV was dark and silent, and Justin was asleep. The clock said it was past midnight.

"Hey." Sean shifted gently, trying to get out from behind Justin. "Sorry, but I need to pee, and I'm aching all over."

"*Mmph*." Justin grunted in protest, but he moved, sitting up and rubbing his eyes. "Bed's more comfy."

"Uh-huh."

They stumbled sleepily to Justin's room, and Sean went into the bathroom to empty his bladder and brush his teeth. When he came out, Justin was sitting on the edge of the bed, dressed only in his boxers and socks.

Sean hovered awkwardly for a moment, unsure whether he should stay or go and make up the sofa bed.

"Make yourself useful. Get in and warm it up." Justin made the decision easy as he stood, stretching. His ribcage lifted, belly concave as he yawned on his way to the bathroom.

So Sean stripped down to his underwear and did as Justin asked. By the time Justin came back, Sean was almost asleep again. Justin burrowed in behind him, snaking a chilly hand over Sean's waist. Their skin warmed quickly where they were in contact, and the heat lulled Sean into sleep. The last thing he remembered before drifting off was Justin's hand stroking his belly, like someone petting a cat.

CHAPTER THIRTEEN

Justin woke to a hard dick pressed up against his arse. He wriggled back against it, but Sean didn't respond, so Justin guessed he was still asleep. He shifted his hips again as his own cock thickened and filled.

He wondered what the etiquette was for waking a not-boyfriend with a blowjob and figured there might be consent issues. He had no clue what was going on in Sean's head, and he knew they needed to talk about things soon.

Christmas was over and they just had two more days before Justin would be back at work and this perfect little bubble of stolen time together would be over. Reality would crash in like an unwelcome guest at a party—and then what?

He pushed those thoughts away, preferring to concentrate on the now. Sean was still hard, and he stirred in his sleep as Justin moved again, deliberately letting Sean's erection settle in the crack of his arse. Damn, why hadn't they taken their boxers off before getting into bed last night?

Justin pushed the waistband of his underwear down so he could get his hand around his dick. He teased himself with lazy strokes, relishing the slow build of arousal that heated his skin and drew sweat to the surface.

"Are you doing what I think you're doing?" Sean's voice was a husky whisper in Justin's ear that made his cock throb in his grip.

"Depends on what you think I'm doing."

Sean reached around and wrapped his hand around Justin's. Justin bit back a gasp as Sean's fingers slid between his, adding to the friction.

Sean was moving too now, grinding against Justin's arse in a way that must feel good for him. It would feel even better with a few adjustments.

"Hang on." Justin reached for the drawer by the bed and passed a tube of lube back over his shoulder. "Here."

"Um… what about a condom?"

"Not to fuck me. Just… rub off on me like this." Justin shoved his underwear down further. "Or stick it between my legs if you want."

Sean took his hand away and shuffled around behind Justin for a moment. The bedclothes rustled, there was the snap of a cap, and then he was back. Skin on skin, slippery with lube, his cock skated up Justin's crack with a squelching sound that made them both laugh.

"I think I might have overdone the lube a little." Sean reached around, and with his wet fingers, he started to play with Justin's nipples.

"Better than getting friction burns on your dick," Justin said breathlessly as Sean's fingertips sent spikes of sensation from his nipples to his groin. He fucked into his fist, pushing his arse back against Sean's dick before thrusting forward again.

They managed to find a rhythm that worked. They panted and laughed their way to orgasm, distracted by the sticky sounds of the lube, but only enough to slow them down a little. Sean came first, pressing tight against Justin with a groan as his cock pulsed and spilled in the small of Justin's back. The hot splash on Justin's skin made Justin moan too, his arm working furiously as he jerked himself to the finish.

Afterwards they made a half-hearted attempt to mop up, but the sheets were a mess. Still reluctant to get up, they lay in a damp, sated tangle. Justin lay on his back with Sean in the crook of his arm, one leg thrown possessively over Justin and tracing his fingers over the smooth skin of Justin's chest.

Everything felt so achingly right, like this was exactly where Justin was meant to be. A fierce surge of honesty rose in him, and he couldn't contain it anymore. "This doesn't feel like pretending. This feels real."

Sean's fingers stilled, and Justin's heart pounded in his ears like a drum as he waited an unbearable few seconds for Sean to respond.

"Yeah," Sean finally said. "It does to me too."

Justin let out a long shaky breath, dizzy with relief that they were in agreement about that, at least.

Sean started to move his hand again, making ticklish trails that distracted and comforted all at once, giving Justin the courage to keep going.

"I don't think I was ever pretending. Not really." He captured Sean's hand and twisted around so they were facing each other, bare knees bumping. He needed to see Sean's face, and he needed Sean to see him. To see that he was telling the truth. "I love you, Sean. I've been in love with you for years."

Sean's eyes flew wide. "I had no idea. I thought a crush, maybe… but nothing more." A shadow crossed Sean's features—guilt and discomfort. Justin wanted to kiss it away, but now wasn't the time.

"I put a lot of energy into making sure you didn't know. You were my best friend, Sean. I didn't want to screw that up by making it obvious I had a gigantic crush on you. Especially when I thought you were straight. I tried to forget about you. I dated other guys. But I never stopped loving you."

Sean swallowed, his face tense. He closed his eyes for a moment, then opened them again and held Justin's gaze. "I love you too."

"Like a friend?" Justin pressed.

Sean shook his head. "Like a boyfriend."

Justin's heart beat faster as excitement rose, but he didn't want to hope too hard. He needed to be sure. "How long have you felt like this?" he asked. If it was only a recent thing for Sean, Justin wasn't sure what that would mean. He might change his mind as quickly as this had begun and Justin couldn't bear that.

"Since you started going out with Will at school. Before that, I knew I was attracted to you, but I was so fucking jealous of him. Knowing that he got to touch you in the way I wanted, that he got to connect with you in a way I couldn't because I was too scared to be honest. It killed me." His voice was thick. "And I hated myself for being such a fucking coward."

Justin reeled at this revelation. Pieces of their shared history slotted into place in a new pattern, explaining things he'd never understood before. "I always wondered why you didn't like him. I thought you were just jealous because I was spending time with him instead of you."

"That didn't help. But no, there was way more to it than that. I thought I'd missed my chance with you. That summer, at the end of Year Twelve, I wanted to tell you. I came so close a few times, but fear of my dad finding out if we started something stopped me. And then you started seeing Will and it was too late."

"But after you came out, why didn't you say something then?"

"When? When you were going out with George at uni? Or Conrad after him? Or after you'd started seeing Andy? There was never a time I could have said it without risking our friendship. I was afraid if I admitted I was in love with you, it would make it too hard for us to carry on being mates. Anyway, it's not like you told me either."

"Yeah," Justin said with a sigh. "I guess I always figured if you liked me that way, you'd have said something when we were younger. So there didn't seem any point in mentioning it after you came out. I thought it would only make things awkward."

Sean's face relaxed into a tentative smile. "So we were both idiots, then?"

Justin smiled too. "That's one way to look at it. Or you could be charitable and say we did what we thought was best at the time."

They stared at each other, goofy grins on both their faces. Sean cupped Justin's cheek and moved forward for a kiss. Short, but sweet enough to feed the hope swelling in Justin's heart.

"Now what?" Sean asked when he drew away again, his face serious.

"I want to be real boyfriends," Justin said decisively. "No more pretending—although the pretending was fun."

"I want that too."

Justin breathed a massive sigh of relief. "Oh, thank fuck."

Sean frowned, not looking nearly happy enough for someone who'd just agreed to be boyfriends with the person he'd been in love with for years. "How will it work if I end up getting a job that's hundreds of miles away? I mean… I could turn down an offer if it's too far out of London, I suppose. But beggars can't be choosers."

"We'll make it work." Justin squeezed Sean's hand, lacing their fingers together and gripping tight. "Bloody hell, Sean. We've waited this long to finally get a shot at this. I'm not going to let a bit of distance stop us. We can see each other every weekend, and modern technology gives us multiple ways to stay in touch in between visits. We'll find a way." There was no doubt in Justin's mind that they could do this. He wasn't letting Sean slip away now they'd finally got to this point. "Now, we have a whole weekend to get used to being real boyfriends before I go back to work on Monday. Where do you suppose we should start?"

"With breakfast," Sean said. "Then I could do with some fresh air. It's probably still too icy to run, but I fancy a walk. Then another movie marathon?"

"You gonna stay awake this time?" Justin grinned.

"If you let me watch *The Avengers* instead of musicals, yes."

"Deal. And then is it my turn to get fucked?"

Sean's eyes darkened. "I think that seems fair."

Justin spent all day on Monday trying to hide his bubbling-over happiness at work. When his colleagues asked if he'd had a good Christmas, he replied in the affirmative but didn't give anything away.

It had been the best Christmas ever, but the details were far too precious to share.

The only person he told was Jess.

"So, me and Sean are together now," he said casually over their lunchtime coffee.

Jess choked, eyes bulging as she nearly sprayed latte all over the table. "What?" People turned to stare at her, so she lowered her voice to a fierce whisper. "Oh my God. When? How? And that's totally awesome, by the way. He seemed really nice."

"It happened at Christmas. Turns out he's always liked me too, and we finally got our act together."

Jess went starry-eyed, clenching her napkin against her chest. "That's so romantic. Why don't things like this ever happen to me?"

"I'm just lucky, I guess." Justin finally let the smile he'd been holding in all day spread over his face. "Really lucky."

His luck held.

Sean was waiting for him when he got home, excitement written in every line of his body. He jumped up, running to hug Justin as soon as he got through the door of the living room.

"Hi." Justin hugged him back. "That's quite a greeting. Did you miss me?"

"No. Well, *yes*, obviously… but I've got news. I've been waiting to tell you all day. I didn't want to text." Sean drew back, grinning like a loon. "I got a job offer, and it's in London!"

Relief and happiness poured over Justin like sunshine. For all his brave words before, he'd been afraid Sean would have to move away and of what that might mean for their shiny new relationship. "That's awesome. Fuck, I'm so glad you get to stay."

"Yeah, me too. I mean… I can look for a place of my own, but I'll try and find somewhere close."

"No you bloody won't!" Justin gripped his shoulders, then doubt shot through him. "Unless you want your own place? Because I'd rather you stayed here."

"Yeah? I guess I thought maybe it was too soon—"

"For fuck's sake, Sean. We've been in love with each other for years. It's not too soon. I'm in this for keeps. Stay. Please?"

"Okay." Sean's voice was husky and his lips curved in a sweet smile that made Justin's heart swell. "If you're sure."

"I'm sure." Justin reeled Sean in and they hugged again. He closed his eyes and they prickled with happy tears. He opened his eyes to blink them away, then caught sight of something over Sean's shoulder that made him burst out laughing.

"Been having fun while I was out?"

"Huh?" Sean pulled back, brow furrowed. Then he turned and followed Justin's gaze. "Oh. Yeah," he said sheepishly.

The two gibbons hung from the curtain rail by their arms. They faced each other, nose to nose. The black one's legs hung down, unattached, and the golden one had its legs wrapped around the black gibbon's waist.

"Is that a hint? A suggestion for what to do later?" Justin chuckled. "Because I'd be up for that."

"We don't have a bar to hang from."

"Yeah, but you could hold me up against the wall if you think you're strong enough."

"Only one way to find out." Sean grabbed Justin around the waist and lifted him.

Justin clung to him, laughing again as Sean stumbled back under his weight, crashing down on the sofa with Justin in his lap.

"Maybe not, then." Justin slid his hands into Sean's hair. "But we could do it like this instead."

"So many possibilities." Sean put firm hands on Justin's hips, holding him close. "Maybe we should make a list."

"Sounds good to me."

Justin dipped his head for another kiss and smiled against Sean's lips as Sean kissed him back. It was hard to believe Sean was his now, but Justin figured he had plenty of time to adjust. Sean wasn't going anywhere.

CHAPTER FOURTEEN

Sean finally got around to phoning his dad on New Year's Day. Sitting on Justin's sofa, with Justin's hand held tight in his, Sean waited for the call to connect.

"Hi, Dad. Happy New Year."

The silence at the other end of the phone was broken by a surprised "Sean?"

"I don't think there's anyone else who calls you Dad, unless you've got something to tell me." Sean joked, trying to relieve the tension.

"How are you? *Where* are you?"

"I'm home—I mean, back in the UK." But Justin's flat *was* Sean's home now. He was still getting used to that.

"Been back long?"

"A couple of weeks. Sorry I haven't been in touch before, but I've been busy getting settled. Finding work... somewhere to live."

"You could have come back here if you'd needed."

Sean raised his eyebrows, glancing at Justin who frowned and mouthed, "What?" as he was only getting half of the conversation. Maybe Sean should have put it on speaker.

Sean leaned in close, their heads almost touching, so Justin would be able to hear his dad. He swallowed, searching for the courage to be honest. "Yeah? I wasn't sure how welcome I'd be if I came home. We didn't exactly part on good terms before I left."

His dad cleared his throat, voice gruff when he replied. "I know. I…. It was a lot to take in. You blindsided me. I would never have guessed."

"I've always been good at pretending," Sean said.

Justin nudged him and squeezed his hand. "Yeah, you are," he muttered.

Sean turned and met Justin's grin. He smiled back.

"Is there someone with you?" his dad asked.

"Yeah. I'm with Justin."

"Are you staying with him?" His dad's voice was carefully neutral.

Sean gripped Justin's hand tight. "Um, yeah, about that—" He took a deep breath. "—I'm living with him. Me and Justin are together now. Like… *together* together. I need you to know that. I know you don't like me being gay, but it's who I am, and it's not going to change." His voice faltered, a lump in his throat making it hard for him to get the words out, but he persisted. "I'd rather have your blessing, because you're my dad, and you're the only family I've got. But if you can't accept this, accept *us*… then that's too bad. Because I'm happy—I'm *really* happy—and I'm not going to let anything or anyone spoil this for me."

There was a long silence. Sean listened to his father's harsh breathing down the line, holding his own breath as he waited.

"Bloody hell," his dad finally said, but his voice held no rancour. Then, surprisingly, he huffed out a chuckle. "I suppose I should have seen this coming. You and that boy were always inseparable. In and out of each other's houses, spending all your time together."

"You didn't like it," Sean said.

"No." His dad let out a sigh. "But you're a grown man and you're free to make your own choices. Even if I don't understand them, it's not my place to try and tell you what to do with your life now. Listen, Sean, I did a lot of thinking while you were away. I didn't try saying it in an email because I'm not good with expressing myself that way. But I thought about you and what you'd told me and about your mother and what she'd think of it. And I realised that all she would want would be for you to be happy. She wouldn't have cared about who you loved, only that you found someone who was right for you." His voice cracked.

Sean's eyes prickled and flooded, his vision swimming as tears filled his eyes. He felt light, as though a crushing weight had been lifted from his chest. "Yeah. I think so too."

"So... I'm sorry for not handling this better before you left, but I want to make it up to you now. Come and visit. Bring Justin if you like. If this is serious, then I need to get used to it."

"It's definitely serious." Sean gave Justin a sidelong grin, and Justin beamed back. His eyes were looking rather moist too.

They went to visit Sean's dad on the second weekend in January.

On the train, Sean stared out of the window. Even after that surprising and wonderful conversation with his dad, Sean was incredibly nervous about meeting him face-to-face with Justin there as his boyfriend.

Sean's knee jiggled with tension. Justin's hand was a reassuring weight on his thigh, but he seemed to sense Sean's need for silence and to respect it. This was one of the things Sean loved best about this new relationship with Justin. The parameters might have changed, but the friendship that formed the foundations was rock solid. They knew each other so well. Justin could tell how Sean felt without asking. Sean could feel the unconditional support radiating from him like the comforting warmth of a fire.

When they arrived at the station, they paused by the taxi rank outside.

"It's only about fifteen minutes. Can we walk?" Sean asked, hoping the exercise might help burn off some of his nerves.

"Course."

They walked close but not touching, treading the familiar streets of their childhood. Past their old primary school, past the park where they used to kick footballs and throw Frisbees, past the climbing frame where Justin fell and broke his wrist after hanging upside down so long his knees gave out.

When they reached the house where Sean had grown up, he felt swamped by so many memories. He hesitated near the gate and turned to Justin, needing to take some strength from him.

"You ready?" Justin licked his lips nervously. His blond hair was almost hidden by a black beanie and his nose was pink from the cold.

"Nearly." Sean took both of Justin's gloved hands, holding them up between their chests as he pressed in close and kissed Justin on the lips. Right there in the street where he'd grown up. No more pretending. He was out and proud where anyone could see him—except his dad. The hedge hid them from the front windows, and Sean couldn't help being glad about that. He didn't want to push his dad too far on what he hoped might be the first of many visits as a couple. "Okay, let's go."

He kept hold of one of Justin's hands as they approached the front door.

"You sure about this?" Justin squeezed his hand.

Sean wasn't sure if he meant the handholding specifically or the whole visit. But the answer was the same either way. "Yes."

The electric *ding-dong* of the bell hadn't changed since Sean was a child. His heart lodged in his throat as he saw the shape of his father through the frosted glass panel. And then the door opened, and he was standing there, smaller than Sean remembered him, with a nervous smile on his face that gave Sean hope that this was going to be okay.

His dad's gaze flickered between them, down to their joined hands and back. His smile didn't slip, and Sean relaxed a little more.

"Sean. It's good to see you. You too, Justin." He nodded at Justin.

"Hi." Justin let go of Sean. He took a step forward, offering his hand to Sean's dad, who shook it.

"Come in," Sean's dad stood aside to let them in. He laid a hand on Sean's shoulder as they crossed the threshold, patting it awkwardly as he added, "Welcome home, Son."

Sean's place was with Justin now, but for the first time in years, he felt like he might be truly welcome in his childhood home again. More than ever, this New Year was a time of new beginnings. Possibilities stretched out before him, and happiness unfurled in his chest, like fragile shoots seeking sunlight. He smiled, releasing Justin's hand to pull his father into a brief hug. "Thanks, Dad."

About the Author

Jay lives just outside Bristol in the West of England, with her husband, two children, and two cats. Jay comes from a family of writers, but she always used to believe that the gene for fiction writing had passed her by. She spent years only ever writing emails, articles, or website content.
One day, she decided to try and write a short story—just to see if she could—and found it rather addictive. She hasn't stopped writing since.

Connect with Jay
www.jaynorthcote.com
Twitter: @Jay_Northcote
Facebook: Jay Northcote Fiction

More from Jay Northcote

Novels and Novellas
Cold Feet
Nothing Serious
Nothing Special
Nothing Ventured
Not Just Friends
Passing Through
The Little Things
The Dating Game – Owen & Nathan #1
The Marrying Kind – Owen & Nathan #2
Helping Hand – Housemates #1
Like a Lover – Housemates #2

Short Stories
Top Me Maybe?
All Man

Free Reads
Coming Home
First Class Package

Audiobooks
Cold Feet
Nothing Serious
Nothing Special
Nothing Ventured
Not Just Friends
The Little Things
The Dating Game – Owen & Nathan #1
The Marrying Kind – Owen & Nathan #2

Share Your Experience

Thank you for reading *What Happens at Christmas*. Reviews help other readers find books. Please consider leaving a review for this story.

Printed in Great Britain
by Amazon.co.uk, Ltd.,
Marston Gate.